Shattered Hearts

Book Two of the Hearts Trilogy

Sabrina Wagner

Copyright © 2016 by Sabrina Wagner
Shattered Hearts
Book Two of the Hearts Series

Cover art by Jill White at Jillzeedesign.com

All rights reserved. This book or any portion thereof may not be reproduced, transmitted, or used in any manner whatsoever without the written permission of the author except for the use of brief quotations in a book review.

This book is a work of fiction. All characters and storylines are the property of the author, and your support and respect are appreciated. Names, characters, businesses, places, and incidents are either the products of the author's imagination or used in a fictitious manner. Any resemblances to actual persons, living or dead, or actual events is purely coincidental. The author acknowledges the trademarked status of various products referenced in this work of fiction, which have been used without permission. The publication/use of these trademarks is not authorized, associated with, or sponsored by the trademark owners.

The following story contains mature themes, strong language, and sexual situations. It is intended for adult readers 18+.

Stay Connected!

Want to be the first to learn book news, updates and more? Sign up for my Newsletter.

https://www.subscribepage.com/sabrinawagnernewsletter

Want to know about my new releases and upcoming sales? Stay connected on:

Facebook~Instagram~Twitter~TikTok
Goodreads~BookBub~Amazon

**I'd love to hear from you.
Visit my website to connect with me.**

www.sabrinawagnerauthor.com

Books by Sabrina Wagner

Hearts Trilogy
Hearts on Fire
Shattered Hearts
Reviving my Heart

Wild Hearts Trilogy
Wild Hearts
Secrets of the Heart
Eternal Hearts

Forever Inked Novels
Tattooed Hearts: Tattooed Duet #1
Tattooed Souls: Tattooed Duet #2
Smoke and Mirrors
Regret and Redemption
Sin and Salvation

Vegas Love Series
What Happens in Vegas (Hot Vegas Nights)
Billionaire Bachelor in Vegas

Table of Contents

Prologue
Chapter 1: Kyla
Chapter 2: Tyler
Chapter 3: Kyla
Chapter 4: Tyler
Chapter 5: Kyla
Chapter 6: Tyler
Chapter 7: Kyla
Chapter 8: Tyler
Chapter 9: Kyla
Chapter 10: Tyler
Chapter 11: Kyla
Chapter 12: Tyler
Chapter 13: Kyla
Chapter 14: Tyler
Chapter 15: Kyla
Chapter 16: Tyler
Chapter 17: Kyla
Chapter 18: Tyler
Chapter 19: Kyla
Chapter 20: Tyler
Chapter 21: Kyla
Chapter 22: Tyler
Chapter 23: Kyla
Chapter 24: Tyler

Chapter 25: Kyla
Chapter 26: Tyler
Chapter 27: Kyla
Chapter 28: Tyler
Chapter 29: Kyla
Chapter 30: Tyler
Chapter 31: Kyla
Chapter 32: Tyler
Chapter 33: Kyla
Chapter 34: Tyler
Chapter 35: Kyla
Chapter 36: Tyler
Chapter 37: Kyla
Chapter 38: Tyler
Chapter 39: Kyla

Prologue

Shattered Hearts

My heart was ripped from my chest,
Leaving a gaping hole where it used to be.
It had been thrown to the ground,
Where it shattered into a million pieces.
I kneeled on the floor and scraped up the pieces.
I tried putting them back together.
But they didn't fit quite right.
The pieces were jagged and ugly.
Some were forever missing.
My heart was a mangled mess.
Time and time again the pieces fell apart,
Leaving me to start over and try once more,
To put my shattered heart back together.

Chapter 1
Kyla

"Does he know?" Tori asked.

I shook my head and started sobbing again. Both of us were soaked from the falling snow and the chill was setting in.

"Are you going to tell him?"

"Now? Are you kidding me? After what I just saw, I can't!" I choked on my tears.

Tori nodded. "I'm gonna call Chris to get the truck and we're going to get the fuck out of here." Tori pulled out her phone and started to dial.

I grabbed her arm. "You can't tell Chris I'm pregnant."

She gave me sad eyes. "Okay, I won't tell him. But you and I are going to talk about this later. I can't believe you kept this from me." She called Chris and he quickly pulled up next to us a few minutes later. Tori climbed into the back with me and held me as I cried on her shoulder.

"What the fuck is going on?" Chris looked at us with concerned eyes. "Why is she crying?"

Tori looked at him and shook her head. "Just drive. There's a hotel a couple miles up. We're staying there for the night."

Chris pulled up to the hotel. Tori and I grabbed our bags from the truck, while Chris checked us in. When we got to the room Tori handed me my bag. "Go change out of those wet clothes, and I'm going to talk to Chris for a minute."

I took my bag, went into the bathroom, and shut the door. Sliding down the wall, I leaned against the bathtub. I was numb. This couldn't be happening to me. I heard Chris and Tori talking in hushed tones outside the door.

"What the fuck is going on, Tori?"

"She caught Tyler fucking some other girl."

"Are you serious? What the fuck is wrong with him?" Chris's voice was filled with disbelief.

"She walked in on them in one of the bedrooms upstairs," Tori explained.

"I gotta be honest, I'm having a hard time believing this. I know he loves her. Is she sure it was him?"

"Chris, she's sure."

"I'm going to find him. You girls stay here. He's got some explaining to do."

I heard the door slam shut and I jolted upright from my position on the floor. A soft knock came at the door. "Kyla, sweetie, are you alright?"

"I'll be out in a minute," I answered. I quickly changed out of my wet clothes and threw on a pair of sweats and Tyler's hoodie. It was the only other shirt I brought.

I opened the door to the bathroom and found Tori, already changed, sitting cross-legged on one of the beds. I crawled up and sat across from her.

Tori took my hands in hers. "How far along are you?"

I looked down at our joined hands. "About six weeks," I breathed out.

"Six weeks and you haven't told him yet?"

I looked back up at her face that was filled with disappointment. "Tori, I couldn't. I couldn't tell him before the Rose Bowl. He would have been totally distracted. I was planning on telling him tomorrow."

"You still can. I think you should," she said definitively.

I shook my head. "I'm not telling him. We're obviously not together anymore."

"Yeah, but he's still the father." She took a deep breath and looked away. Then she stared me down. "Are you keeping it?"

I looked at Tori with shock. "Yes! I'm keeping our baby."

"And you're not going to tell him? He's going to find out eventually."

"I'm not going to tie him down with this. I want him to want me for me, not because of a baby he didn't plan on."

"He has a right to know!" Tori exclaimed.

"He gave up that right tonight!" I shouted at her. "He destroyed us tonight! I'm doing this with or without your support. Although, it would be easier with it."

Tori leaned forward and gave me a huge hug. "I don't agree with your decision, but I'll support you. We've been friends since we were eight. I love you like a sister." She sat back up. "Does this mean I'm going to be an aunt?" She smiled at me with excitement.

"Of course, you are! He or she is going to need their Aunt Tori." I took her hands in mine again. "Please don't tell anyone. I'll do it in my own time. Chris is too close to Tyler and my parents will try to talk me out of it. No one can know right now."

"Okay, I'll keep your secret. I don't like to keep things from Chris, but I'll do it for you."

"Thank you." I breathed out a sigh of relief.

"Do you want to talk about what happened tonight?" Tori asked.

"There's not much to talk about. He cheated." The tears started pouring down my cheeks again. "I trusted him. I always trusted him. He betrayed me! God, I'm so stupid. I should have seen this coming. I was so blind," I ranted. "I thought we were solid. I don't know how to live without him. I don't know how to breathe without him."

"Maybe this was all a misunderstanding," she said hopefully.

I rolled my eyes at her. "I didn't misunderstand seeing his dick in someone else. What? It just accidently fell into her?"

"You need to talk to him," Tori said softly.

"I will. But not tonight. Tonight, I'm just going to wallow in my own misery. How do I even face him after this?"

Chapter 2
Tyler

I ran back upstairs and grabbed my clothes off the floor. Madison was standing next to the bed getting dressed. She was short, and she had long blond hair like Kyla's. I gave her a death glare and shook my head as I pulled my shirt on.

"What? You're mad at me? You're the one who grabbed me." She glared back.

"I don't even fucking know you! I thought you were someone else!" I shouted.

"And that's my fault? You're an asshole, you know that?"

I stood with my hands on my hips and let out a frustrated breath. "Look, I'm sorry. It's not your fault. It's mine."

"I'm sorry your girl saw us." Once she was dressed, she started to leave the room. She stopped and turned to me before walking out the door. "Listen, if things don't work out with her, give me a call." And with that, she was gone.

I rubbed my hands over my face in frustration. *How did this even happen?* I sat on the edge of the bed and rested my arms on my knees, holding my head. This was a colossal clusterfuck! How in the hell was I going to fix this?

"Hey." Cody popped his head into the room.

"Hey," I answered.

"For what it's worth, I tried to stop her. I tried to get to you first."

"Why didn't you stop *me*?" I questioned. "You know I wouldn't have done that if I wasn't drinking. We're supposed to watch out for each other."

Cody sat down on the bed next to me. "Honestly, I didn't know. I saw you go upstairs, and I saw the blond hair and assumed it was Kyla. I didn't realize it wasn't until Kyla found me and asked where you were. I'm sorry, man." I could tell he really was sorry.

"Don't be. It was my own fucking fault," I answered. "How could I be so drunk that I didn't realize it wasn't my own girlfriend?"

"From the back, that girl was a dead ringer for her. What are you going to do?"

"I don't know, man." I shook my head. "How do I say, *Sorry I stuck my dick in someone else*, without it sounding totally lame? I don't think that's going to go over very well."

Cody let out a low laugh. "Probably not." Cody stood and walked toward the door. "I'm here if you need to talk." Then he knocked on the door frame and left me with my own thoughts.

If she hadn't been so damn late, I wouldn't have started drinking like that, and this would have never happened. *Good job, Ty. Nice way to blame her for you being an ass.* I groaned. Now what? My phone buzzed in my pocket. "Hey, Chris," I answered.

"You still at that party?" His voice was clipped.

"Yeah, I'm getting ready to leave."

"Meet me out front. We need to talk." He hung up. *Fuuuuck!*

I checked my missed calls and texts. There were about a dozen from Kyla saying they were running late because of the snowstorm. I groaned again in frustration, ran my hands through my hair, and put my shoes on. I went downstairs and out to Chris's truck. I opened the door and slid in without even looking at him.

"You wanna explain to me why Kyla's sitting in a hotel room with Tori, crying her eyes out?" He was pissed and had every right to be.

I ran my hands through my hair again. "I fucked up! That's why!"

"Obviously. Care to explain?"

"Dude, I don't even know. Arrrgh!" I looked at Chris who waited for my explanation. "I don't know. I was waiting for you guys to get here. I started doing shots. I got drunk. I thought I saw Kyla, so I went up behind her and took her upstairs to one of the rooms. It was dark. One minute I'm inside what I think is my girl, the next she's standing in the doorway. That's when I realized it wasn't Kyla, but some chick I don't even know named Madison." I held my head in my hands and just shook my head.

"That's fucked up!"

I glared at Chris. "You don't think I know that!" I practically screamed at him.

"How, after being with Kyla for three years, did you not know?"

"I was drunk! I still am, but this has sobered me up pretty fast. I'm telling you this chick looked just like Kyla from behind. I never looked at her face until it was too late."

Chris rubbed his hand over his face. "I don't even know what to say. I believe that you didn't mean for this to happen, but it did. Now what?"

"Take me to see her. I have to talk to her," I pleaded.

"No way, man! You're still drunk and nothing good can come of that. I'm taking you back to your dorm. Sleep it off. Then come see her in the morning."

"You're right. I know you're right. But not seeing her is killing me. I need to get her back. This is going to destroy us."

"I'm not gonna lie, it might. But just wait 'til the morning." Chris shifted his truck into drive and headed toward the dorms.

I stumbled back to my room and crashed down on the bed. This night did not turn out at all like I had planned. I looked at her smiling face staring back at me from the picture on my desk. Then I pulled open the drawer and took out the small box inside. I flipped it open and looked at the diamond ring I was supposed to give her tomorrow. I *was* going to propose. I snapped the box closed and threw it on top of my desk. Fuck! How did everything get so messed up in less than twenty-four hours? Yesterday, playing in the Rose Bowl, had been one of the best days of my life. And now. Everything was a disaster!

I fell asleep that night thinking about only one thing. How was I going to get my girl back?

Chapter 3
Kyla

Chris came back about an hour later. He threw his keys on the dresser and just shook his head.

"Did you see him?" I asked.

"Yeah, I saw him. He's a mess."

"Good! What did he say?" I questioned further.

Chris looked at me with sympathetic eyes. "He said it was an accident. He's drunk. He didn't know what he was doing. He thought it was you."

"Yeah right! He knows every curve of my body. How could he not know? It doesn't even make sense." I huffed.

Chris plopped down in the chair. "I know it doesn't. But I have to tell you, I think he's telling the truth," he admitted. "He was really drunk. I've never seen him like that."

I crossed my arms and stood from the bed. "Are you defending him?"

Chris threw up his hands. "I'm not defending him. I'm just telling you what he said."

"So, what now?" Tori asked, looking at me. "Are you going to talk to him?"

"I don't know." I sat back down on the bed and looked at my hands. I looked at the ring on my finger that was his promise to me. He had given me his heart and I had given him mine. Now it felt like my heart had been smashed with a sledgehammer and was a bloody mess. It hurt to breathe. My chest ached. "I don't know what to do." My eyes filled with tears again and they began to fall down my cheeks. I wiped them away with the back of my hand.

"Well..." Chris looked at me with apologetic eyes. "Ty wanted to come here tonight, but I wouldn't let him. I took him back to the dorms, but he's coming here tomorrow morning. You need to talk to him. At least hear him out."

Tori came over and put her arm around me and pulled me into a side hug. "You're right," I said. "I should hate him right now, but I can't. I love him so much. I don't know how we move on from this. What do you think I should do?"

Tori looked me in the eye. "You have to talk to him."

I knew she was alluding to the baby. I needed to tell him, but I just didn't know how after everything that happened.

"How can I take him back and keep my self-respect? What if he's been cheating on me all along?" I asked.

Chris let out a disgusted grunt. "I can't even believe you just said that. You should know better."

"I thought I did and look what happened tonight," I shot back at him.

"I know him. He hasn't been cheating on you. And deep down, I think you know that too," he insisted.

"I don't know what to think anymore," I confessed. "I thought we would be together forever, now I'm not sure of anything."

After talking late into the night, we went to bed. I was physically and emotionally exhausted. Chris and Tori slept in one of the beds. I slept in the other. I had never felt so alone. My mind wouldn't shut down. Before all this happened, I was going to tell him about the baby. Our baby. I was supposed to tell him tomorrow. I thought we were ready to take the next step together. Get an apartment together. The baby was unplanned, but I had hoped he wouldn't be upset. I knew it would change everything, but I really thought we could handle it. Now I didn't know what was going to happen. I thought back to the day my life changed.

It was the second week of December. I was over a week late. Shit. We had been careful. We always used a condom. Tyler was insistent on it. He didn't want a baby right now.

I went to the store and stared at all the boxes of tests sitting on the shelf. I didn't know which one to buy, so I bought three different ones. I had the clerk put them in a paper bag, just in case Tori was home when I got there. Stuffing the bag in my backpack, I headed home to find out what my fate would be.

When I got back to my dorm, Tori wasn't there. I went into the bathroom and opened the first box. Quickly reading the directions, I peed on the stick and waited. I never wanted to fail a test so bad. Please be negative, I pleaded. I picked up the test and saw a plus sign. SHIT! I opened the next two boxes and took those tests. Same results. I shoved everything back into the bag and stuffed it into my backpack.

I sat down on the toilet seat and tears ran down my face. What was I going to do? I couldn't get rid of it. Despite the fact that this was unplanned, this baby had been created out of love. How was I going to tell Tyler? I needed to wait until football season was over, that much I knew. I would tell him then and everything would work out. Right?

What if he was pissed? What if he thought I planned this? What if he didn't want our baby? He had made it very clear that he didn't want kids anytime soon. All the "what ifs" ran through my head. For now, I would keep the secret. All the "what ifs" would be answered soon enough.

In the meantime, I'd plaster a smile on my face and pretend that my life wasn't about to change.

Now what do I do? I cried myself to sleep, trying to figure it out.

Chapter 4
Tyler

I fell asleep but slept restlessly. When I woke, I had one hell of a headache. I looked over at my desk where there were two aspirin and a bottle of Gatorade. Cody must have left it, knowing I was going to feel like shit in the morning. I jumped out of bed, immediately regretting the fast movement, and hopped in the shower. I needed to get to Kyla and try to explain last night. All I could do was try.

I drove to the hotel and texted Chris that I was there. He texted back the room number, and I made my way up. My palms were sweaty as I rode the elevator up to the third floor. I wiped them off on my jeans and stuck my hands in my pockets. When I got to the room, I took a deep breath and knocked.

Chris opened the door.

"Hey, man. Tori and I are going to get breakfast. Text me when you're done." They walked out of the room hand in hand. Tori gave me a look I couldn't decipher. It was either sympathy or pure disgust. I braced myself, not knowing what I was walking into.

Kyla was sitting in the middle of the bed. Her eyes were puffy and rimmed with red. I didn't have to ask to know that she had been crying. I crawled up to sit across from her. "Hey, baby." She closed her eyes and turned her head to the side. Her lips pressed together, in an attempt to hold back the sob stuck in her throat. My heart broke just looking at her.

I didn't know where to start, even though I had rehearsed my words a thousand times on the way here. Seeing Kyla sitting across from me, the sadness in her eyes, everything I had practiced vanished. I decided to start with what was in my heart. "I'm so sorry, Kyla. I don't know if you can ever forgive me." I took her face in my hands and looked deep into her green eyes.

She stared back at me, the life in her eyes gone and replaced with a blank stare. "You cheated," she said. "And worst of all, I saw it. I saw it all." Her voice was emotionless.

"I didn't mean to," I tried to explain. "I thought it was you."

"Really?" she scoffed. "I'm pretty sure you know what my body feels like. What I fucking look like!" She reached up and grabbed my hands from her face and threw them back at me.

"Kyla, please just listen to me," I begged her. "I started drinking with the guys. I know it was irresponsible…"

"Irresponsible! Irresponsible? Are fucking kidding me? It's not like you forgot to feed your goldfish. You screwed someone else!" And then the dam broke, and the tears flooded down her cheeks. "How long has this been going on?" she questioned.

What? How could she think that? "I haven't been cheating on you. Please… let me explain. I really thought it was you I was leading up those stairs. I was so drunk, and I missed you so much. It was dark and all I could think about was getting inside you. YOU! You're the only one I want. Have ever wanted!" I leaned forward and wrapped my arms around her small shoulders that were shaking as she tried to stifle her crying. Her arms hung limply at her sides, not returning my embrace. My eyes welled with my own unshed tears. I was going to lose her.

She turned and looked at me, her eyes narrowed in anger. Anger I deserved. "Did you go down on her?"

"No." I shook my head.

"Did she go down on you?"

"No." These questions were killing me, but I deserved every one of them.

"Did you use a condom?"

"Yes." I groaned internally at her question, as the reality of what I had done sunk in deeper.

"Did you come? Did she?"

"No, it didn't get that far. I swear," I answered honestly.

"What was her name?" She kept it coming, as her anger turned to sadness again.

"Does it matter? What matters is that it was a mistake. It meant nothing."

"Nothing to you. Everything to me." The tears poured down her cheeks. I reached up and wiped them away as I caressed her face.

"I didn't mean it like that. I would never hurt you on purpose. I love you so much. Please say we can fix this."

"You know what hurts the most?" she asked. I just looked in her sad eyes, not knowing what to say. "I can't stop loving you. I should hate you, but I can't. I can't! I don't know how to live without you. You are *everything* to me and I feel like you've ripped my heart out and stomped on it, breaking it into a million little pieces."

"I know," I said, dropping my head in shame.

"Do you? Because it feels like I'm bleeding from the inside out and I don't know how to stop it. I gave you everything. EVERYTHING!"

"Ky, please." I took her small hands in mine. She tried to pull away, but I wouldn't let go. I couldn't. "Please give me a chance to fix this. I don't know how to live without you either. You are *my* everything. You're my reason for breathing." I took her hands and placed them against my chest. "You're the reason my heart beats."

Her eyes softened. I leaned forward capturing her bottom lip and pulling it into my mouth. Pushing my tongue between her lips, our tongues twisted together. I kissed her deeply and let my hands tangle in her hair. She reached up and grabbed the back of my head, pulling me into her. I leaned her back on the bed and hovered above her, framing her face with my hands. "Please, forgive me," I whispered.

My hand slid under her shirt, rubbing against her slender waist. I tentatively moved my hand up to cup her breast and rubbed my thumb over her nipple. She gasped and bent her head back. I kissed down her neck and pushed her shirt up. I pulled the cup of her bra down and sucked her nipple into my mouth. "I only want you. I only need you," I whispered to her.

She whispered back, "I only want you. I need you."

I uncovered her other breast and swirled my tongue around her nipple, sucking and nipping it. "Please, let me taste you. I need to know you're mine." She would hear what our bodies said, even if my words failed me. I was desperate for her. I needed her to remember how perfect we were together.

Her hands moved to the waistband of her sweats, and she started to ease them down her hips. I put my hands over hers and slid her pants down over her ankles, rubbing her soft skin along the way. She pulled her shirt up over her head as I rubbed my hands back up to her thighs. "You are beautiful, Kyla. You're the only one I've ever wanted. I need you to believe that."

"I want to believe it. Make me believe it, Tyler. Show me you still want me," she rasped out. God, her voice was sexy when she was turned on.

"I still want you. Always." I put my head between her thighs and licked up and down her folds. I ran my tongue down to her wet pussy and lapped up her essence, savoring the taste that was uniquely her. I worked her over slowly, taking my time, making her feel everything. Licking up her folds again, I ran my tongue along her clit before sucking it into my mouth. She began to writhe on the bed, pushing her hips up into me. I stuck two fingers into her wetness and pumped them in and out, curling them to find that sweet spot that made her go crazy.

"Ty... please... don't stop!" I kept sucking her clit and pumping her with my fingers, until she came long and hard. She let out a high-pitched scream when she orgasmed, as I pumped her through it, feeling her clenching around my fingers. "Oh my god... fuck that was good!" she gasped.

I crawled back up her body and captured her lips with mine, kissing her deeply. "I want to give you a lifetime filled with orgasms like that. Orgasms that make your toes curl and your body tremble. Give me that chance. Let me make love to you. Let me remind you how good we are together."

"Please... make love to me," she whispered.

I grabbed a condom and quickly stripped out of my clothes. I kneeled between her legs and pulled her up to me. I wrapped my arms around her hips and under her ass, as she wrapped hers around my neck. I looked into her sorrowful green eyes and spoke the truth. "I love you so much. I don't want to lose you."

"Show me," she said.

Not wanting to waste a second, I kissed her with everything I had, trying to prove to her what she meant to me. I lay her back down and slid my dick into her slowly, pushing deeper, making Kyla feel every long inch of me. Putting my weight on my hands next to her head, I slowly slid out. Slowly in, slowly out. Until she begged me, "Ty... faster... harder. Fuck me like you mean it. I need you to show me."

It was all I needed to hear. I went to my knees and pulled her hips to me. I thrust into her hard and fast, her moans driving me to make her pleasure my only objective. I gave her everything I had. "Ky... come for me, baby!"

She reached her hand down and rubbed her clit frantically, as I continued to thrust into her. She threw her head back and her pussy gripped me tighter, pulsing around me. We fell over the edge together, the ecstasy washing over us.

I hoped it was enough to prove to Kyla that she was the only one for me. I knew she really didn't want to let go of what we had, no matter how she was feeling.

Collapsing next to her and pulling her to my chest, I ran my fingers through her long hair and kissed the top of her head. "Never doubt my love for you, Kyla. I can't live without you."

Chapter 5
Kyla

I laid there in Tyler's arms feeling so many things. Love. Hope. Betrayal. Fear. Pain. Making love to him didn't help sort out my feelings. I was so conflicted. I loved him. That much I could not deny, but I also couldn't forget what I had seen. Mistake or not, it devastated me. I wasn't sure I could get past this.

He turned my face to his. "Stay with me tonight and tomorrow night, before we have to start classes again."

I was honest with him. "I love you, Ty, but I'm not sure I can get past this. What I saw," I shook my head, "…I can't unsee. I can't get the images of you with her out of my head."

"I know what I did was wrong. Believe me… I know. But I can't lose you because of a drunken mistake. Just stay with me. Try to forgive me."

"It's not the forgiving I'm having a hard time with. I know you didn't mean for this to happen. It's the forgetting. I can't just erase my memory." I knew it wasn't what he wanted to hear, but it was the truth.

"I get it," he said sounding defeated. "I really want to try though. I want to replace what you saw with things you won't want to forget."

"I'd like that. I can't make any promises, but I'll try." I didn't want to give up on what we had built together for the last three years. And there was our baby to consider. I wanted him or her to have two parents who were together. Who loved each other. I needed to do this for our unborn child. The words I needed to tell him were on the tip of my tongue. Keeping this secret from him made me feel so guilty. I knew he deserved to know, but how could I find the right time? I made my decision right then. I would stay with him tonight and, if things went well, I would tell him tomorrow. I had to be sure we were solid.

Tyler ran his fingers along the side of my face. "What are you thinking?"

"I'm thinking I want to stay. Are you sure though? That's like three hours of driving to take me home and come back."

He smiled down at me. "I'm sure," he said. "I'll drive a hundred hours if it means you'll stay."

"Then I'll stay. Can you take me to the mall though? I'm going to need some other clothes. My jeans from last night are still wet and I don't want to wear sweats for the next two days."

"I'll take you anywhere you want, Ky.

I took a deep breath and let it out slowly. "Okay. Let's get dressed. Can you text Chris while I fix myself up?"

I went to the bathroom, shut the door, and looked at the girl in the mirror. What did it say about me that I was willing to take him back so easily? Did this make me pathetic? A push over? Stupid? I didn't know. The only thing I knew was that I couldn't give up on him. On us. I believed him. Was I naïve? Was this going to bite me in the ass? Time would tell.

I brushed through my hair and braided it down my back. I put on some concealer to hide the dark circles under my eyes and applied a little mascara and some blush. I looked in my bag and realized that in addition to jeans and a shirt, I was going to need clean underwear too. Tyler would just have to suffer Victoria's Secret with me.

I heard the door of our room open, and then hushed voices. I couldn't make out what was being said, but I was sure they were talking about me. I wondered what Tori and Chris were going to think about my decision. I opened the door, ready to face their judgement.

"Can I talk to Kyla alone for a minute?" Tori asked. I couldn't tell what she was thinking, but I knew I was about to find out. Tori always said what was on her mind, even if she knew I wouldn't like it.

"Yeah, we'll just wait in the hall," Chris answered. He grasped Tyler by the shoulder and led him out of the room.

Once the door shut, Tori grabbed me by the hand and led me over to the bed to sit down. "Well?"

"We talked... and... well... okay, don't judge." I dropped my head in shame.

"And what?" Tori questioned. "Please tell me you didn't."

I looked back at her, cringed, and blurted it out in a steady stream of word vomit so she couldn't interrupt. "And next thing you know he was kissing me, and then I was naked, and then he put his mouth all over me, making me orgasm. Then he made love to me." I finally took a breath and sighed. "And it was so good."

"Kyla! You were supposed to talk to him, not let him fuck you senseless."

"I know! I know! I don't know how it happened." I threw up my arms and folded my hands on top of my head.

"So, how much actual talking did you do?" she asked. "What are you going to do?"

"I told him I would try to get past this. I believe that he didn't mean for this to happen. I just don't know if I can do it. I can forgive, but forgetting is going to be hard. I have to try. For all of us." I patted my still flat stomach where our unborn baby sat.

"Did you tell him?"

I shook my head. "Not yet. I'm going to stay with him for the next couple of days. If things are going well, I'll tell him tomorrow."

Tori took a deep breath and closed her eyes. "Just tell him about the baby. The sooner the better."

"What if he gets totally pissed? I mean, it's not like this was planned." I couldn't help agonizing. If I was being totally honest with myself, I was afraid of what his reaction would be. Yeah, I didn't want to tell him before the bowl game, but now I was just stalling because I was scared.

"That's a chance you're going to have to take. And if he does get pissed, then I guess he's not the man you thought he was. Plus, he really can't get mad at you after the shit he just pulled," Tori reassured me.

"I guess you're right. I'm going to tell him. Tomorrow. Everything is just too raw today. We have a lot more to talk about."

"Talk being the key word. Talk, not fuck. Pull it together and do what needs to be done," Tori lectured. Then she looked at me with concern. "Are you sure you want to stay here. Chris and I can take you home."

"I'm sure," I said. "I need to give this a try."

"Well, if things go bad, and I hope they don't, call me. I'll come get you."

I leaned in and gave Tori a hug, wrapping my arms tightly around her. "Thank you. Thank you for being my friend. And thank you for keeping my secret. And thank you for always being there for me." My voice broke as my emotions took over again. Stupid hormones!

Tori hugged me back just as tightly. "I love you, girl."

"I love you too," I choked out.

"Keep me in the loop, okay? Call, if you need me." She stood from the bed, pulling me with her. "Come on. The guys are waiting."

Chapter 6
Tyler

Chris led me out to the hallway so the girls could talk. I leaned against the wall and hung my head, waiting for Chris's judgement. Being sober amplified the embarrassment I felt about what I did last night. I looked up at Chris. "Man, I'm sorry I put you in this position between Kyla and me. You've been a good friend and I shit on that last night. I don't want you to have to choose sides."

"You fucked this up pretty good. I've known Kyla a long time and seeing her like that last night... it was fucked up." He shook his head at the memory. "But I also know you're a good guy and you love her. As fucked up as the situation is... I believe you didn't do it on purpose."

"Thanks. I just don't want this to screw things up between you and Tori. I already know whose side she's on."

"I think you'd be surprised. Tori is, of course, always going to be there for Kyla, but she also knows how good you've been for her. You helped her to open up. You taught her how to actually enjoy life and live a little. Tori's rooting for both of you. She wants you guys to fix this. So, what happened? Did she forgive you?"

"Kyla said she can forgive, but not forget. I don't blame her. I can't even imagine how I would feel if I had walked in on her with someone else. I'd want to rip his fucking head off." Just thinking about that pissed me off. Would I be able to forgive her? Forget what I had seen? It would devastate me. Just like I did to her. If she took me back, I would never take Kyla for granted again. This whole situation made me realize how much I depended on her. Loved her. Needed her. "Anyway, she's going to stay with me the next couple of nights so we can try to move past this."

Chris looked at me incredulously. "How in the world did you get her to agree to that? Last night, I swear, she wanted to chop your dick off and shove it down your throat. She was a fucking mess all night."

I shrugged my shoulders. "I begged and pleaded and reminded her how good we are together." I quirked my eyebrow at him.

"You didn't!" He looked at me and realized I wasn't joking. "You fucking did, didn't you? You're a fucking dog, you know that?" He let out a low laugh. "You've got balls, I'll give you that."

"I was desperate, man. I can't just let her walk away," I explained. "Anyway, things are still not settled. She's hurt and I have a lot of work to do to earn her trust back, but I'm going to try like hell over the next couple of days. Wish me luck?" I held my fist up for him to bump.

Chris returned the gesture. "You must have a magic dick because I didn't even think you'd make it this far. Good luck, man."

"Thanks for not ripping me a new one last night or running over me with your truck. Thanks for being cool."

Chris crossed his arms and shrugged. "Shit happens, right? Just fix this with her."

I leaned my head back against the wall. "I'm gonna try."

The door to Kyla's room opened. She and Tori walked over to where we were standing. "I'm ready to go," she said. I took her bag from her and threw it over my shoulder. She gave Chris and Tori hugs. "Thank you for everything."

Tori gave me a hug and whispered in my ear. "Treat her right. Fix this. She needs you more than you know right now."

"I will," I assured her. Tori didn't seem as angry as I thought she would be, and I took that as a good sign.

I put my arms around Kyla's shoulders and led her to the elevator. We rode down to the lobby in silence. When we got to the car, I opened her door, and she slid in. I didn't really know what to say to her. I had already apologized, but it wasn't enough. It would never be enough. I would spend a lifetime making sure she never doubted me again. I got in, started the car, and turned up the heat. I took her hand and threaded our fingers together. She leaned back in the seat and closed her eyes. "I don't know what to say to you," I admitted. "Tell me how to make this right?"

"I don't even know." She let out a heavy sigh. "I just want to forget this ever happened, because honestly, I can't even believe we're in this situation. I feel like it's a bad dream and I just want to wake up." A single tear ran down her cheek. "You have to promise me that nothing like this will ever happen again. I'm barely hanging on. I can't ever do this again."

"It won't, baby." I squeezed her hand tightly, brought it to my mouth, and kissed her fingers.

"Let's go to the mall, so I can get some clothes. Oh, and by the way, I need underwear too, so we'll have to stop at Victoria's Secret." She gave me a small smile. "And I'm kind of hungry, but I'm exhausted too."

"How about this?" I suggested. "Cody left this morning for a few days. We could pick up some food, take it back to my room, and take a nap. I know you didn't sleep well last night and neither did I. Then a little later I'll take you to the mall."

Kyla shifted in her seat and leaned her head against my shoulder. "Sleep would be great," she said drowsily. She wrapped her arms around my bicep and snuggled in. "No sex though, just sleep."

I kissed the top of her head and started driving. "Just sleep. I promise." I stopped at a drive-thru, picked us up some breakfast sandwiches, and headed toward the dorms.

When we got to my room, we sat on the bed and ate. "Can I borrow of one your shirts to sleep in?" Kyla asked.

I went to the closet, grabbed one of my long-sleeved shirts, and handed it to her. "This okay?"

She held it to her face and breathed in. "Perfect," she said. "It smells like you." Kyla stripped out of the sweatshirt she was wearing, which was also mine, and pulled on the other shirt. She slipped off her sweatpants since my shirt was huge on her. It hung down and hit her mid-thigh. She was damn adorable in my clothes.

I yanked my shirt off over my head and replaced my jeans with basketball shorts. I had to remind myself—no sex, just sleeping. Pulling back the comforter, I sat on the bed and patted the space next to me. Kyla walked tentatively toward the bed and sat, her shoulders slumped, and her head hung down.

I hated the fact, that for the first time in our relationship, everything was weird between us. I hated that I caused it. I hated that the smile I loved was missing from her face. I hated that I did that to her. I hated the fact that a diamond engagement ring was sitting in my desk drawer, and I couldn't put it on her finger. Not now.

Kyla reached over and grabbed the picture from my desk. She stared at her own face, then turned the picture over and removed the back of the frame. She took out the other pictures tucked into the back. She looked at each one, a faraway look in her eyes, like she was remembering. When she got to the one of us out in the water, where her legs were wrapped around my waist and we were staring into each other's eyes, a small smile spread across her face. "I love this one," she said softly. "We were so in love."

"We still are," I said as I brushed back some loose curls that had fallen from her braid. "We're going to get through this," I promised. I scooted back on the bed and pulled her with me. I laid down, tucking her back to my front. I molded my body around her tiny frame, my arm went around her waist, pulling her tight to me. She pushed her hips back into my mine and tangled our legs together. It felt amazing holding her like this. I kissed the top of her head and took in her scent. "I love you, Kyla O'Malley."

"I love you too, Tyler Jackson." Her voice cracked, and I felt a tear hit my arm that was under her head. A piece of my heart broke, knowing I was the source of her sadness. I wrapped her tighter in my arms. This was where she belonged. Here with me.

Chapter 7
Kyla

I woke several hours later and was immediately hit with a wave a nausea. I quickly slipped out of Tyler's arms and ran to the bathroom, barely making it to the toilet before the contents of my stomach came up and my abdomen violently convulsed. I kneeled on the floor in front of the toilet and rested my arms on the bowl. Another wave of nausea hit and more came up. My forehead beaded with sweat, and I felt lightheaded.

Just then, a light knock came at the door. "Ky, are you okay?" The door opened, and I quickly flushed everything down. He kneeled next to me and rubbed my back gently. "Are you sick?"

I lifted my head and attempted a weak smile. "I'm not sick. I'm…" Now was not the time. "I just think that food didn't settle well with my stomach. I'm fine," I lied. I hated myself for being a liar.

"Are you sure? You don't look so good," he questioned.

"Yeah. I'm fine," I said with a little too much sharpness. I pushed myself to my feet and went to get my toothbrush. I brushed my teeth and rinsed my mouth. Tyler looked at me with concern. "Really, I'm okay," I said softer this time. It was so much harder to pretend that I wasn't pregnant with him standing there.

"If you say so. Do you want to get dressed and I'll take you to the mall?"

"That would be great," I said, grateful for the change of topic. I changed back into my sweats and hoodie, threw my shoes on and we were out the door. It was freezing outside, and I shivered while waiting for the heat to kick on in the car.

"Why didn't you bring a coat?" Tyler reached over and ran his hands up and down over my arms trying to warm me up.

"I did. I left it in Chris's truck. I didn't want to take it into the party and then I forgot about it." I shivered.

Tyler frowned. "Let me go get you one of mine," he offered.

"No, I'm good. Let's just go, the heat will kick in soon," I insisted.

We got to the mall, and I made quick work of finding a pair of jeans and a couple of tops. We walked hand in hand as we headed toward Victoria's Secret. It was nice to do something normal, and it seemed like the tension between us was easing. "You want to come in with me, or wait out here on the bench?" I asked, as we stopped in front of the store.

"Depends, will you model for me?" he teased as he twirled my hair in his fingers.

"Whatever you want," I teased back. I was loving the flirty banter between us.

"Then I'm definitely coming in." Tyler pulled me forward into the store. He didn't seem embarrassed at all by the racks of bras and panties on display. "How about these?" he said, holding up a barely-there thong.

I grabbed his wrist and pushed it down. "Really?"

"What? These would look sexy as hell on you." He put them down and picked up another thong. "So would these," he said with a big smile.

"Fine," I said and grabbed both thongs with amusement.

"Are you getting bras to match?" he whispered in my ear.

I felt the heat and wetness pooling between my legs. I had promised myself no more sex, but I couldn't help the way my body reacted to him. "Would it turn you on if I did?" I whispered back.

He nodded.

I smiled, looking through the rack trying to find my size. I found a 36C that matched. I wasn't huge on top, but with my small frame, they were plenty. I held it up for Tyler to see. He ran his fingers over the lace cups and groaned. I took that as a *yes* and looked for a bra to match the other thong. Finding what I needed, we moved to the register. I leaned up toward his ear. "You'll have to wait 'til we get home, for a private viewing."

"You're not helping," he said as he readjusted himself.

It felt good knowing I affected him this way. We'd always had a strong sexual attraction to each other. I'd never wanted to be with anyone other than Tyler. After all that we'd done, I couldn't imagine that anyone else would measure up.

Then it hit me. We were each other's first and only. Tyler couldn't say the same thing anymore. I was not his "only" anymore. Even if he didn't come, as he claimed, he'd been inside of someone else. I wondered how I measured up.

We walked out of the store and my demeanor changed as I thought about this. My brain was going crazy, fighting with my heart.

"You wanna get a pizza on the way home?" Tyler asked.

"Sure." My monosyllabic response earned me a quirked eyebrow.

"Do you want to eat out or take it back to the dorm?"

"Dorm is fine." He hated the word "fine", and I seemed to be using it a lot lately.

We bought a pizza in the food court and headed back to the dorm. My mind was still spinning, as I weighed my options. Get over the cheating or get over Tyler. Both options seemed impossible. Fucking fuck! I leaned my head on the window on the drive back, stuck in my own head.

When we got back to his room, he threw the pizza on the desk. He sat on the edge and crossed his arms over his chest. "Okay, spill it! Something's got you all pissed off again. I thought we we're having a good day, and now you're all sulky and shit."

I grabbed my purse and headed toward the door. "Maybe this was a mistake," I muttered.

He took three steps forward, grabbed me by the shoulders, and spun me around to face him. "What was a mistake? The last three years?" he asked angrily. Then his voice softened. "I don't believe that." He ran his fingers along the side of my face.

I looked in his eyes. "You don't get it, do you? How do we pretend like nothing happened? Go back to being us? You were my first and only. I was yours. Now I'm not! And it fucking hurts! It's fucking breaking me!" I tried to keep my voice from cracking but failed miserably. "Now I feel like I'm competing for you. Was she better than me? Prettier than me? Did she have bigger boobs than me? I just don't know what to think. And I can't stop thinking about it!" The tears ran freely down my face.

Tyler wrapped his arms around my shoulders and crushed me to him. I held him and just cried into his broad chest. I let it all flow out. It was ugly, and I knew it. I sobbed and sobbed, letting the sadness consume me. He just held me and let me get it out.

When my tears subsided, Ty cupped my face with both hands. "You're still my only one, baby. The only one who matters. The only one I can't live without. The only one who makes me feel whole. I'm so sorry I did this to us, but I can't take it back. I wish I could. I wish I knew how to make you believe me. I'll never be able to apologize enough to you, but I'll keep trying until you forgive me. Do you want this to work?"

I nodded my head. "More than anything. I don't want to lose you. And I feel like I have."

"You haven't. I'm right here." He held up my hand with his ring and kissed it. "You still have my heart." Then he flashed me his dimples. "And for the record, your boobs are perfect."

"Yeah?"

"Yeah." He leaned forward and kissed me deeply. His hands skimmed down my back until he reached my ass. He picked me up, and I wrapped my legs around his waist. He carried me to the bed and sat down on the edge, with me still on his lap and pushed my hair out of my face. "If this is going to work, you're going to have to try to let it go. I know it's asking a lot, but it's the only way."

"I know. And I'm really going to try. I want… no… need… this to work. I love you so much."

"Don't run away from me. When things get tough, talk to me."

I rested my head on his shoulder and just enjoyed his warmth, the way his arms felt around me, and the way he smelled. Tyler was my home. Nothing felt as good as this.

Chapter 8
Tyler

I wanted to hold Kyla like this forever. I thought about the ring in my desk drawer. I still wanted to ask her to marry me, but I didn't want her to think it was because of what happened. I didn't know what the answer was, but something told me to wait. Now was not the time.

"Our pizza is getting cold," I said.

Kyla untangled herself from me and crawled off my lap. "Pizza first, then fashion show?" she asked.

"You said no sex," I reminded her.

"I said fashion show, not sex." She smiled coyly at me.

"Yeah, but when I see you in that bra and panty set," I groaned. "I'm gonna want sex."

"Maybe I'll change my mind. I guess we'll just have to wait and see." She was teasing me. I had agreed to "no sex", but honestly, I wanted it. Always wanted it with Kyla.

We opened the pizza box, and I devoured four slices. I was starved. Kyla barely ate one. She picked, more than she ate. "Is your stomach still upset? You've barely eaten."

She shook her head. "I'm just being careful. I don't want a replay of before." She walked over to my mini-fridge and grabbed a bottle of water. "You want something?"

"I've got other things in there besides water, you know?" The fridge was filled with both alcoholic and non-alcoholic drinks. She was a diet Coke-aholic. She said that if she didn't have her caffeine, she got headaches, so I always had a few cans in there for her.

"No, no, water is fine." She waved me off. "So, fashion show?"

"Are you going to tease me? You know this is going to give me a hard-on."

"Just lay back and relax. I'll make it worth your while." She picked up her Victoria's Secret bag. "Are you sure Cody's not coming back tonight?"

"I'm sure. It's just you and me."

Kyla walked to the bathroom. "I'll be right back." She went in and shut the door.

I lay back on the bed and threw my arm over my eyes. I knew she wanted this to work as much as I did and hoped I was doing a good job convincing her to stay. We had so much history between us, I could barely remember my life before her. She was pure. The best thing in my life. How could I have been so stupid?

The bathroom door clicked open. I sat back on the edge of the bed to take her in. Kyla stood with one arm up on the door frame the other on her hip. I had always thought she was sexy, but as the years went by, she'd gotten sexier. She had become curvier and more filled out. She'd become curvier and more filled out. Gone from being a seventeen-year-old girl to a woman. My woman.

"Well?" she asked. "What do you think?"

"I think you need to come closer, so I can get a better look." I crooked my finger, beckoning her to me.

She walked toward me, swaying her hips slightly. I looked her over from the top of her blond head down to her pink painted toes. She was sexy as fuck! The cups of her bra were all lace, showing her nipples through the fabric. They were hard and beautiful. The thong sat high on her hips, the lace barely covering her most intimate area. I motioned for her to turn so I could see the back. The string from the thong was practically invisible, showing me her toned, rounded ass cheeks. I ran my hands softly over them. She turned back so she was facing me. "Well?" she questioned again. "Is it to your liking?"

"You look sexy as sin, Ky." She came closer, stepping between my legs. I ran my hands up from her hips to her tits. They filled my large hands, and I ran my thumbs over her nipples. "Either your boobs are getting bigger, or this bra pushes them up more." I gave them a slight squeeze, massaging them gently. "I think they're definitely getting bigger."

Kyla lowered to her knees in front of me. She locked her eyes to mine and started to undo the button on my jeans. "I want you, Ty." She slowly slid my zipper down and reached inside to free my long, hard cock. I helped her push my jeans down my hips, giving her better access. I lean back on my hands and let her work her magic. She licked the head of my dick agonizingly slow, swirling her tongue under the edge. "Do you remember the first time I blew you?" she whispered. I nodded my head, unable to speak. "This is going to be so much better," she promised.

She slipped her lips down over my cock and took me all the way to the back of her throat. Shit, that felt good! My eyes rolled back into my head, as she rubbed my dick along the roof of her mouth, her hand pumped me hard all the way down to the base. She opened her throat and took me deeper still, squeezing me every time she swallowed. Her other hand was on my balls, gently rubbing and exploring. The sounds she made vibrated and intensified the pleasure. She kept taking me deeper, swallowing, pumping me harder, swirling her tongue up and down my shaft. My balls tightened, and my dick twitched. "I'm gonna come, baby!" I gasped. She didn't stop but moved faster. My hips bucked up off the bed and I grabbed the back of her head, fisting her hair. "Oh my, god!" All my muscles tightened, and I let go. I exploded, as an intense orgasm rocked through my body. She never released her lips and pumped every last drop from me, swallowing it all down. I collapsed back on the bed. I was spent.

Kyla kissed up my stomach and laid next to me on her side. Her head rested on her hand, as she looked at me. She took her other hand and ran it down my face and under my chin. "Holy shit, Ky," I said, as I tried to catch my breath. "What the fuck was that?"

"That was me giving you a mind-blowing orgasm." She smiled down at me seductively.

I pulled her on top of me and she giggled. I rubbed my hands down her back and grabbed her ass. She placed her hands on my shoulders and kissed me passionately. She nipped at my lips and pushed her tongue deep into my mouth. I moved my hands to the back of her head, not letting her escape, as I returned the kiss with eagerness. I loved kissing her like this. It felt like we were the only two in the world and we were starved for each other.

She broke the kiss first. "I just wanted to make you feel good." She rubbed her nose against mine.

"That pretty much electrified my whole body. You always were an overachiever." I placed a gentle kiss on her forehead. I eased her to the side and pulled my shirt up over my head. I took my jeans off but left my boxer briefs on. I lay back down and pulled Kyla into my side. She wrapped her arm around me and snuggled into the crook between my shoulder and chest. She took her leg and threw it over my waist, gripping my thigh with it. I held her tightly and rubbed small circles on her back. We were wrapped in a tight little cocoon of each other.

Kyla sighed in contentment. "This is my favorite place in the whole world. Right here in your arms."

"It's where you belong." What I asked next was a risk, but I needed to know where her head was at. "Have you given any more thought to what we talked about at Christmas?"

"Which part?" she questioned.

"About us moving in together."

"I have."

She wasn't giving anything away. "And?" I pressed her for more.

She sighed. "It's complicated. MSU doesn't offer my program and I'll have an internship for graphic design next winter. You can't transfer, and neither can I. The NFL scouts have been looking at you, and I can't give up on a program I have three years invested in. Our lives are about to get very complicated." She drummed her fingers on my chest nervously.

"Complicated doesn't mean impossible. What if we found a place in the middle? We'd both have to drive a little bit, but it's doable. Plus... you could give me more mind-blowing orgasms if we lived together." I groaned.

Kyla swatted at my chest. "So, this is about sex?" She laughed, lifting her head to look at me.

I grabbed her hand and kissed her palm. "No. It's about being closer to you. Taking the next step. Sex is just an added bonus." I waggled my eyebrows at her. Then I turned serious again. "One day I want to marry you, buy a house, and have a family with you."

"One day? What does that mean?" she said softly and dropped her head back to my chest.

"Hey, look at me." I put my fingers under her chin and turned her face back to mine. "I'd marry you tomorrow if you'd let me. And when we're done with college and have our careers set, we can think about kids. I'm not ready for that yet. It wouldn't be fair to you, me, or a baby."

I saw something shift in her eyes and then it was gone. "No, you're totally right. You have so much going on between football and classes. The last thing you need to worry about is a baby." She had a hint of disappointment in her voice and her eyes got glassy.

I ran my fingers through her hair. "What's going on with you? I'm not saying no. I'm just saying not right now," I assured her. "You know how I feel about this. We've talked about it."

"I know. I'm just... I guess I'm just a little emotional lately."

"That's my fault. I'm sorry, Ky." She'd been up and down all day. I couldn't blame her. She was still trying to deal with what had happened last night. That was on me.

"It's not your fault. I need to learn how to deal with shit. Be realistic." Her forehead creased, and her eyes narrowed in thought. "I know it's not the plan. But, seriously, would it be that bad if I got pregnant? I mean we love each other, right?"

"Kyla, it's not about how much I love you. That's not in question." I sighed. Where in the hell was all this coming from? I thought she was on board with the plan. I wasn't mad, but this conversation was a little frustrating. "How the hell would we deal with a baby? We barely have time for each other now, let alone adding a baby to the equation. That would be a disaster. I want to enjoy my time with you, and only you, for a while." I kissed her on the tip of her nose, and she dropped her head back to my chest.

"Can we talk about something else?"

Chapter 9
Kyla

What in the hell was I going to do now? He was pretty clear about his feelings. *That would be a disaster.* His words rung through my brain over and over again. They stung like a swarm of bees invading my heart.

That would be a disaster.

You know how I feel about this. That would be a disaster.

He had just made the decision for me. I guess I was going to do this on my own. I was going to enjoy this time with him and then I would have to leave. Put some distance between us. It was going to kill me to do that, but I was going to have this baby, with or without him. I just wished he was more open to it. He had goals and plans. I did too, but I wasn't going to turn my back on our baby. Maybe in time he would accept it, but not now.

Tyler interrupted my thoughts. "Did you fall asleep on me?"

"No. Just thinking," I answered. I turned and faced him again. "So, you like the new lingerie?" I asked. I knew what was coming, but he didn't, so I tried to lighten the mood. I didn't know when I was going to have to cut our ties, but I didn't want to waste a minute of our time together. I loved him. This was going to annihilate us. And shatter my heart beyond repair.

"Like it? I love it!" He rubbed his hands along my ass and gave it a little squeeze.

"I'm glad. I love to see you happy. Do you even know how much I love you? Always remember that I would not be who I am without you." I kissed his lips feverishly. Memorizing everything. This was the beginning of good-bye.

I straddled him, rubbing my hands along his chest. "You're my Labraweiler."

Tyler looked at me in confusion. "Your what?"

I had never told him what Tori had said to me all those years ago. "Tori told me a long time ago that I always dated guys that were cute, like a Labrador Retriever. She said I needed a Rottweiler. We decided I needed something in between, sweet as can be, but a little bit bad. A Labraweiler. You're my Labraweiler. Everything I ever needed." I ran my nails along his chest. "You've been the best thing that ever happened to me." I forgot about everything that had happened last night and soaked in the here and now.

"Labraweiler? I like it." He smiled and rubbed his hands along my thighs. "I can be sweet, but I'll always be there to protect you. Fiercely. "

"I know. I've always known. From the first day I met you, I knew." I looked at him and memorized those blue eyes. The ones that I got lost in. The eyes that looked into my soul and captivated it.

Tyler ran his hands up my stomach to my tits. He ran his thumbs along my nipples that protruded through my bra. He gently rubbed over the hard tips, pulling me forward and sucking my nipples through the lace. First one, then the other. My boobs were so sensitive, and a shot of lust ran through my body down to my core. I moaned in pleasure.

"You look incredible in this. So sexy." Ty pulled one cup down and swirled his tongue around my peak, then sucked it into his mouth. I arched my back, leaning into his mouth. I wanted more. Needed more. He reached behind my back and undid the clasp of my bra and slid it down my arms. "You are so beautiful. I remember the first time you let me see you. When you dropped your dress, I thought I had gone to heaven. And then, when I saw your tits, I almost came right then." He let out a low laugh.

"We didn't even know what we were doing." I ran my finger from his chin down his neck and to his chest. "But we figured everything out together. Thank you for sharing all your firsts with me." I kissed him again, remembering everything we had experienced together.

Tyler wrapped his arms around my waist and flipped me onto my back. He took my arms and stretched them above my head, clasping my wrists in one hand. "There's no one I would have rather shared them with." This was love. "And there is so much more I want to share with you."

He kissed my forehead, the tip of my nose, down my chin to my neck, and between my breasts. He massaged my swollen breasts and sucked each nipple into his mouth. I arched off the bed as pleasure rocked through my body. No one would ever touch me like Tyler did. No one else could ever possibly make me feel this good. This sexy. This wanted. I wanted to bottle what we had and keep it forever. I used to think we would last forever, now I didn't know if we would last another night. Everything was so complicated, so messed up, so unsure.

Ty kissed down my stomach and swirled his tongue around my belly button. He slid my thong down my legs and over my ankles. He ran his hands up my calves to my thighs and gently pushed them apart. "I'm going to take my time with you." His voice was filled with lust. He ran his tongue up the inside of one thigh and put it over shoulder. Then did the same with my other leg. He kissed from my pelvic bone down to my bare pussy. He ran his tongue between my folds. His touch was exquisite. I lifted my hips toward his face.

"I'm going to make you come so hard. Then I'm going to fuck you slow and deep and when you think you can't take anymore, I'm going to fuck you fast and hard." I let out a moan at his words that had the power to make me forget everything else but him. This man knew my body. How to make me writhe, scream his name, and beg for more. "Do you want that, baby?

Do you want me to make you come? Do you want my cock in your pussy?"

"God, yes! Yes...please! Make me come...I need it!" I was impatient and needy as Tyler began his slow torture of my body. He ran his tongue through my folds again, finding my clit, swiping it with long, lazy strokes. He sucked it into his mouth, teasing it with his tongue. The pressure began to build and left me hanging on the edge, barely holding on. He released my clit and the pressure subsided. I gasped in frustration.

Tyler stuck one finger inside, then two, then three. He stretched me and filled me, as his fingers pumped in and out slowly, then faster. He finger-fucked me hard, pounding into me over and over again. He crooked his fingers inside me, finding that special spot that made me ache for more. I arched off the bed. His hand went to my stomach and pushed my hips back down, not letting me grind into his hand. I threw my head back. "More... more... make me come."

"I will," he whispered. "I'm gonna take care of you. Give you what you want." His thumb stroked over my clit, barely skimming my sensitive nub. Another brush of his thumb and the pressure was building again. My pussy clenched his fingers as I climbed higher, closer to the edge again. I ground my teeth and squeezed my eyes tight. And then it was gone. I felt like a rubber band ready to snap. There was so much tension in my body. I needed the release he was holding from me. "Do you want it now? Are you ready?"

"Yes! I can't take anymore. Please." I begged him. Tyler buried his head back between my legs. He captured my clit with his mouth and sucked hard. His tongue lashed at me, stroking me with the tip. Then he sucked again, pulling and pulling. The pressure became unbearable. My body tensed as every muscle in my body tightened and my whole body arched up off the bed. Tyler gripped the sides of my hips, pulling my pussy to his face, not letting me go. The pressure was almost painful. I felt myself teetering on the edge.

And then I fell over. Pleasure radiated through my body. It started at my core and spread to my toes, raced to my fingertips that gripped the sheets in desperation, and ran down my spine. I bucked off the bed as Tyler's mouth continued its assault. White lights flashed behind my eyes as I shattered into a million pieces. "Tyler! Fuck…Tyler!" I screamed his name.

He rubbed slow, hard circles on my clit, bringing me back down. I gasped for air. My body went limp. "I'm not done with you yet." Tyler slid his boxer briefs off, reached into his desk, and pulled out several condoms. I wanted him to fuck me all night. I was sure he would.

He slid into my wetness as slowly as he had promised. He always took care of me. He wasn't a selfish lover. My pleasure was his pleasure. He hovered over the top of me and rubbed along my clit with his dick every time he pushed in. I was so sensitive. I lifted my hips to meet every one of his agonizingly slow thrusts. The friction on my pussy and clit was making me build again. He pushed in so deep and circled his hips. I came again, and I felt like I was flying. I never wanted to come down. My body clenched Tyler, squeezing his length tight with my walls, making his eyes roll back into his head. His next thrusts were fast and hard. He let out a growl that started deep in his chest and came inside me.

Tyler quickly removed the condom and slid another one on. He went to his knees, pushed my legs to my chest, thrusting in fast and hard. Relentlessly. He slowed, then reached under my shoulders and pulled me to his lap. He never pulled out but stayed deep inside of me. I arched and dropped my head back, as I pushed my tits toward his face. He gave each one attention with his tongue and lips. "I love when you fuck me," I whispered, taking his head in my hands, and looking into eyes. "There's nothing like making love to my best friend. No matter what happens, promise you'll always love me. Promise me forever." Tears welled in my eyes and slipped down my cheeks.

He brushed them away with his thumbs. "I promise I'll love you forever."

I started to move, taking him slowly. I slid up and down his dick and let him fill me. This position forced him deeper. I felt everything. Wrapping my arms around his strong shoulders, I just enjoyed the feeling of him inside me. We were so entwined in each other. There was no him. There was no me. There was just us.

Chapter 10
Tyler

Kyla and I made love all night long. Hard and fast, slow and sensual, we did it all until neither of us could take any more. We finally crashed in the early hours of the morning, exhausted and physically spent. God, I loved her. I tucked her in close to me and slept with her peacefully in my arms.

It was still early when I felt her slip out of my arms. I cracked one eye and watched her move quickly to the bathroom, shutting the door behind her. She was sick again; the retching sound was unmistakable. What in the hell was going on with her? The toilet flushed, and I heard the sink faucet turn on. I wasn't sure what to do. Go to her or pretend I didn't know. If there was something wrong, she would tell me, right? I had to trust her to be honest with me.

The shower turned on. I waited a few minutes, then went to check on her. I quietly cracked the door open and peeked in. She was standing under the scalding water, hands over her face, shaking with her sobs. I pushed the door open further, and she dropped her hands from her face. "You okay, baby?" I questioned.

She managed a weak smile. "I just needed a shower. I smelled like sex."

"I like when you smell like sex, because you smell like me." I grabbed two towels and a washcloth and set them on the bathroom counter. I stripped off my clothes and stepped into the water with her. Taking her shampoo off the shelf, I poured some in my hand and began to lather her long strands. Her hands went to her hair, and I pushed them down. "Let me take care of you."

I massaged her scalp, and she let out a little moan. "That feels so good," she said. Her eyes closed as I rubbed her head and ran my hands down to the ends of her hair. After I shampooed and rinsed her silky, blond strands, I grabbed the washcloth and squeezed some body wash onto it. "I can do that." She reached for the washcloth.

I pulled it back. "Kyla, please let me." I took her one arm and gently washed it, then the other. I rubbed over her full breasts and down her stomach. When I reached between her legs, she flinched. "Sore?"

"A little, but it's a good sore. Reminds me last night wasn't a dream."

"If we move in together, last night can be our everyday reality." I finished washing her back, her legs, and her pretty little toes. "Wrap yourself in a towel and I'll be out in a few minutes."

Kyla stepped from the shower, patted her hair, and wrapped the fluffy towel around her tiny body. I watched as she ran a comb through her long hair. She grabbed her bottle of coconut lotion from her bag and rubbed it into her arms. She put her foot up on the toilet seat and did one leg, then the other. I imagined what our life would be like sharing these private moments on a regular basis. I loved everything about her. I loved watching her when she thought no one was watching. She really was my everything. I wanted to spend my days taking care of her. I always wanted her to feel safe, protected, cared for. I wanted my arms wrapped around her every day. I wanted to share all the little domestic moments of life with her. I wanted to make her my wife.

After last night, I was even more sure. I wanted it all with her.

I finished showering, dried off, and wrapped the towel around my waist. Kyla was sitting on the bed, leaning against the headboard, wearing my shirt she had worn yesterday. My laptop was on her legs. She looked up at me and smiled. "Hey. I was just looking through Netflix. I hope you don't mind that I grabbed your computer."

"It's fine. What's mine is yours. You know that."

"I just thought that it's so cold outside, maybe we could find a good movie."

"Being snuggled up next to you sounds awesome. Why don't I run down to the coffee shop on the corner and get us some breakfast? Do you want the regular? Carmel Frappuccino?"

She scrunched up her nose. "No, I just want a large hot chocolate and a chocolate chip muffin."

"Are you sure? You love that fancy coffee shit." I pulled on my boxer briefs and jeans.

She laughed. "Yeah, I do love that fancy coffee shit, but I'm sure. Hot chocolate would be great." She got off the bed and reached for her purse. I walked over, took it out of her hand and placed it back on the desk. She scrunched her eyebrows at me. "Just because I'm here, doesn't mean you have to pay for everything. I have money."

"I know you do. But would you please just let me take care of you. I want to." She started to protest, and I cut her off by pulling her into my arms and kissing her. I pulled back and stared down at the woman I loved. "Just let me."

"Okay, okay… go get my hot chocolate. Oh!" Her eyes got wide with excitement. "Can you have them put whipped cream on top? With a cherry?" She was so damn cute.

I pulled a sweatshirt over my head. "Hot chocolate, whipped cream, cherry, chocolate chip muffin. Anything else, my love?" I teased her.

"No. That will be all. Off you go." She shooed me out with her hands.

I laughed and threw my hat on my head. "I'll be back in a few." I headed toward the parking lot. It had snowed during the night, not that Kyla and I had noticed. I brushed the couple of inches of snow off my car and drove to the coffee shop.

I opened the door and the bells on it jangled, announcing my arrival. Breathing into my hands and rubbing them together to warm them, I walked to the counter and placed our order. The girl behind the counter quickly got to work making my coffee and Kyla's hot chocolate. I looked around the coffee shop and spotted Madison in the corner with another girl. I pulled my hat down low over my eyes and looked away. Maybe she wouldn't notice me.

When our order was ready, I paid and turned to leave. I couldn't help but to glance back over to Madison's table. She spotted me and gave me a flirty wave. "Fuck," I muttered to myself. I gave her a head nod and walked out of the shop.

I got back in my car, took my hat off, and threw it on the passenger seat. I could have gone my whole life without seeing her again. She fucking waved at me like she knew me. This was not good. If I was out with Kyla and she saw us... I just didn't want to think about it. I was pretty sure Kyla wouldn't recognize her, but I couldn't be fucking sure. Guilt sat in the pit of my stomach and ate away at me. How could I have done that to Kyla? So fucking stupid!

I started the car and hoped that my run in with Madison was fluke. I'd probably seen her a dozen times before and never knew it. It never mattered before. It didn't matter now. She was nothing to me.

When I got back to my room, Kyla was sitting on my bed talking on the phone. Her slender legs hung out from under my shirt, and she absentmindedly ran her finger along the scar on her knee. "Ty just walked in. I'll see you tomorrow. Bye, Tori." She hung up and smiled at me.

"That was quick. Still freezing outside?" She stood from the bed and walked over to take the drinks out of my hands.

"Yeah. It snowed again during the night." I tried to act normal but seeing Madison had me slightly off-kilter. Nervous.

"Really?" She walked over to the window, set our drinks on the desk, and peeked through the blinds. "I love the snow. It's so pretty. I just get tired of it being so cold." She turned away from the window. "Thank you for braving the cold to get me breakfast." She reached up on her tiptoes and gave me a peck on the lips.

I threw the bag with our breakfast on the bed and grabbed her around the hips. "It's hardly a sacrifice when you're my reward."

She snuggled into my side. So sweet and innocent. She deserved better than me. She was willing to take me back and I wouldn't forget that. She had been my rock, my biggest supporter, my best friend for the last three years. And I pissed it away in one drunken moment. Never again.

"What movie did you decide on?" I opened the bag from the coffee shop and handed her the muffin she asked for.

"Thank you. This is exactly what I wanted." She pulled back the paper and took a bite. "Mmmm... so good!" She flopped back on the bed and picked up my laptop. "I couldn't decide. I didn't know what you were in the mood for. Comedy? Drama? Action? What do you think?"

I sat down next to Kyla and kissed the side of her head. "I think you should decide."

Kyla decided on *The Proposal*. I found it ironic that of all the movies, she chose that one. We snuggled close and just enjoyed being together. She laughed so hard during the campfire scene that she could barely catch her breath. I loved watching her like that. Just fucking happy.

After the movie, we talked and spent some quality time together. We talked about our classes for this semester and our goals for the future beyond college. She said that once she got her degree, she wanted to work for an advertising agency doing graphic design, but eventually wanted to run her own company. With the internet and her artistic talent, Kyla's possibilities were endless. I wanted to play pro football. That had always been my dream. She knew that. We could make our two goals work together. I might have to move around for the first couple of years, and her career choice would allow her to move with me. It was perfect really.

By the time late afternoon hit, I was starved. I convinced her to let me take her out on a proper date. There was a new Italian restaurant in town, and I wanted to take her there. She did her makeup, changed into the new outfit she had bought yesterday, and threw on her tall boots. She really was beautiful.

While she was getting ready, I made my decision. I opened my desk drawer and took out the engagement ring. I knew now, more than ever, that I could not live without her. This could be the little push she needed to agree to live with me. To take the next step. To be my forever. I slipped the box in my pocket before we left for dinner.

The restaurant was perfect. The lights were dim, and candles were lit on every table. Soft music played overhead. It was romantic. Kyla's eyes sparkled in the candlelight as we held hands across the table.

We were back to being us. All the awkwardness of the day before disappeared. It was hard to believe that just two days before I had almost destroyed us. And now I was ready to propose.

We just finished dinner and were looking at the dessert menu when all it all went south. I was about to reach into my pocket when someone caught my eye. Fucking Madison! She sauntered over to our table without a care in the world, a wicked smile on her face.

"Hi Tyler!" She beamed at me, putting her hand on my shoulder. "I can't believe I've run into you twice today." Fucking hell!

Madison reached across the table to Kyla. "Hi. I'm Madison." Kyla's eyes narrowed as she ignored Madison's outstretched hand and picked up her napkin instead. Recognition flashed in Kyla's eyes. Madison pulled her hand back, seemingly unaffected.

Kyla threw the napkin back on the table and stared Madison down. "Is there something you wanted?"

"Just wanted to say hello to *our* number one guy," she said in a flirty tone. "I'll leave you two alone." Then she leaned in close to me and whispered in a not so quiet voice, "Thanks for the other night. You were amazing!" And just like that she left. I was speechless. What the fuck just happened?

Chapter 11
Kyla

I was fucking done! "Tyler, I'd like to go home now." I stood up, grabbed my purse, and walked toward the door. It was one thing knowing what had happened, but it was another having it thrown in my face. I walked out into the cold and stood next to Tyler's car.

I knew he would be a while, he had to settle our bill. I waited. The cold barely registered with me; I was so pissed. Madison? Really? Her name was like acid on my tongue. I knew it. As soon as I saw her, I knew it. The look on Tyler's face told me everything. He was uncomfortable, and Tyler was one of the most confident people I knew.

This was the second time he had seen her today? What the fuck? She was gorgeous. Long, blond hair like mine. Bright blue eyes. Long lashes. And big boobs. Like really big! I couldn't compete with that.

Tyler came out of the restaurant and walked over to the car. He didn't say anything, just opened my door. Was he seriously upset at me?

He slipped into the driver's seat. "Kyla, I..."

I held my hand up in his face. "Save it. I don't want to know. I've seen everything I need to see."

We drove back to his dorm in silence. When we got to his room, I started packing up all my shit.

"Kyla, what are you doing?" He was trying to unpack my things as fast as I was packing them up.

I turned and faced him, hands on my hips. "Oh, I'm sorry. Did you misunderstand me? I said I wanted to go home. I thought I was pretty clear." I went to the bathroom to get my toothbrush and anything else that was mine.

"Kyla! Just stop! It was nothing! She's nothing!" He threw his hands up in the air in frustration.

I walked right up to him and poked him in the chest. "Really? Didn't seem that way to me. Is she my replacement when I'm not around?" I knew I was being irrational. But for fuck's sake, how much was I supposed to take?

Tyler grabbed me by the shoulders. He was pissed at my words. "You're overreacting! You're acting like a bitch!"

Well, that was a knife to my heart. In three years, we had never resorted to calling each other names. I felt like I had been stabbed in the chest. My eyes welled with tears. My voice softened, "Then I guess it's a good thing you won't have to deal with me. You know? Me being a bitch and all?" I twisted out of his grasp and finished packing my things.

"Kyla! I'm sorry. I didn't mean it."

"Kind of like you didn't mean to fuck her!" A tear ran down my cheek. "I thought I could do this, but I can't. I can't! I love you, but I can't compete with that." I zipped up my bag and threw it over my shoulder. I faced away from him. I couldn't look him in the eye. "Are you taking me home or should I call a cab?"

He walked up behind me, wrapped his arms around my waist and put his chin on my head. "I don't want you to go. Please stay," he pleaded.

"I can't," I said softly. "I need some time. Some space." I turned and faced him. "If I stay… I just can't. I have to be able to think clearly. And I can't do that here with you."

He lifted my chin with his fingers. "Can't or won't?"

"What's the difference?" I looked away. "I'm not sure we want the same things anymore." I rubbed my hand over my stomach unconsciously, our conversation about babies resurfaced in my mind. This would be easier right? A clean break. I needed to go. "I'll just call a cab."

"I'm not letting you call a cab. I'll take you home."

"It's too far. I just… I don't even know." I was breaking as much as he was. This is what I wanted. Right? An excuse to put some distance between us. I really could get over what happened in the restaurant, but he wasn't ready for this baby. And I wanted it more than anything. Even if that meant sacrificing my true love… my best friend. What else could I do? Maybe one day he would understand… I was doing this for him. For his future and dreams. He deserved everything he had worked so hard for. I had become a complication. He just didn't know it yet.

"It's not too far. I'm not letting you get in a cab with some stranger for an hour and a half. I don't want you to go. But I'll take you if that's what you want."

"I want to go home," I said, dropping my head to my chest. Home used to be wherever Tyler was, but not anymore.

We hardly talked on the way back. It was a miserable silence. What was said was strained and uncomfortable. This was not us. Or it didn't used to be. This was our new reality.

"Kyla, I don't know what to do to prove that it was nothing. I want you and only you," Tyler pleaded.

"Ty, I love you. That will never change. Ever. But this is just too much for me to handle." I sighed. "She's gorgeous. I don't know how to deal with this. I tried, but I can't have it in my face. Maybe you need to explore other options. How do we know we were made for each other when we've never looked beyond each other? I don't know what to do."

"Do you want someone else? Is that what this is all about?" he asked.

"There's no one else. I don't… I'm not going to hold you back and have you regret it later. I'm setting you free."

Tyler huffed. "I don't want to be free. I want you."

"I want you to live your dreams. We can still be friends. I'll always be there for you."

"You're friend-zoning me?" Tyler pulled the car to the side of the road. "I can't just be your friend."

I looked him in the eye and regretted everything I was about to say. "It's friends or nothing."

His eyes narrowed, and his anger seeped through. "You know what? Fuck this! And fuck you for making me feel this way! I tried to make you understand the truth, but you're too fucking stubborn." He pulled back onto the road, going way too fast.

We made it back to Western in record time. He pulled up in front of my dorm, refusing to look at me. "You're home," he said.

I turned and looked at him, my heart breaking. "I love you. I'll always love you." He made no motion to return the sentiment. Just stared forward. I grabbed my bag from the back seat and walked toward my dorm. I was destroyed. Decimated.

He drove off in a hurry. This was the end.

Chapter 12
Tyler

What the hell just happened? Three years gone? Just like that? She friend-zoned me? I was fucking pissed! I thought we had gotten past all the bullshit. The last twenty-four hours were good. No... not good... great! She gave me the best orgasm of my life. We'd made love all night long. I tried to show her that all I wanted to do was take care of her. Being friend-zoned was fucking unacceptable!

I can't believe I called her a bitch, and I can't believe I basically told her to fuck off! That wasn't the way we talked to each other. What was happening between us? I'd never talked to her that way. Never!

Time. Fucking time. If that's what she needed, I'd give it to her. She was being emotional. Irrational. She knew we belonged together. Why was she fighting it?

Fucking Madison, that's why! What the fuck was up with that chick anyway? She was obviously unhinged! Off her fucking rocker! I can't believe she came up to us in the restaurant like that. And thanking me for the other night? Was she fucking insane? Did she not get that it was all one big fucking mistake?

I just drove. I couldn't get out of my own head. I flipped the radio on, hoping to get lost in the music. There was little chance of that happening. "Torn to Pieces" by Pop Evil came on. I went to change the station, but my hand froze on the knob. I listened to the words. My eyes welled with tears. One escaped and rolled down my cheek. I quickly wiped it away. Why the fuck was this happening? I didn't just lose my girlfriend. I lost my best friend. My future wife.

I pulled to the side of the road and lost it. I banged my fists on the steering wheel and then dropped my head to it. The fucking tears rolled down my face. I couldn't stop them. I was shattered. My chest felt like someone had punched a hole right through it.

I don't know how long I sat there. I lost time. I finally straightened up and pulled myself together. This is what it felt like to lose everything. Two days ago, I thought I had lost it all, but I knew then I still had a chance. Now all my chances had been used up. I would have given anything to have her back, but somehow, I knew she wasn't coming back. This really was the end. The realization crushed me.

It was late when I got back to MSU. I flopped down on my bed and pulled the pillow to my face. It smelled like Kyla. My whole goddamn room smelled like her. How was I going to get her out of my head when everything reminded me of her? We made love on this bed not even twenty-four hours ago. I took the picture from my desk and pulled the photos from the back. I looked at the one Kyla had stared at yesterday. She was right. We were so in love. Were? Are? I didn't even know anymore. Somewhere along the way, we broke.

I thought back to Kyla's words. *Our lives are about to get very complicated.* What did that even mean? Loving her was the easiest thing I had ever done. I pulled the box from my pocket and opened it. The diamond sparkled in the light. This was supposed to be my future. I snapped it closed, opened my desk drawer, and shoved the ring way in the back. Out of sight, out of mind. If only it were that easy.

I went to the fridge and pulled out a beer, downing it in a few short gulps, then grabbed another one. I might as well get shit faced. By the time I emptied the fridge of everything alcoholic, my anger had boiled to epic proportions. *It's friends or nothing.* Fuck that! I threw my beer bottle across the room, and it smashed against the wall. That's the last thing I remembered before I passed out.

Chapter 13
Kyla

Thank God, when I got to my room it was empty. I didn't need interrogations. I didn't need sympathy. I didn't need the judgement I knew was coming.

I missed Tyler already. We'd had to part ways many times over the last three years. But this was different. More permanent. We'd never left each other on bad terms. He'd said I was being a bitch. Yeah, I probably was. I had to be. It was the only way he would let me go. And I needed to go. He didn't want this baby. I did.

I went to my closet and pulled down the purple box that held all our memories. I carried it to my bed, sat down, and slowly removed the lid. The last three years of my life were in this box. I pulled out the contents and laid them across my comforter. So many pictures. I looked lovingly at each one. Every picture told a different story. The story of us. My prom corsage, a reminder of the night I lost my virginity. The bottle of sand we had made love on at the lake house that summer. His college football programs from the games where I cheered for him harder than anyone else. The tears trickled down my cheeks. So many good memories.

I gathered everything up and placed it back into the box. I set the box on the desk next to my bed and changed out of my clothes, pulling Tyler's football jersey on. Crawling beneath my sheets, I cried silent tears. I did this to myself. I looked at my phone. Nothing. I don't know what I was expecting. I destroyed Tyler on the way home. Said we should explore other options. Said I only wanted to be friends.

Lies.

All of it had been lies.

It was after one in the morning when Tori finally came in. I wasn't asleep. I was thinking about the last few days, over and over in my head, like a movie stuck on replay. The good. The bad. The ugly. "Oh shit! Why are you home? I thought you weren't coming back until tomorrow?"

"Yeah. Me too." I sighed.

Tori looked at the purple box on my desk and pointed to it. "That's not a good sign." She knew what that box meant to me.

"I was just remembering my life before I fucked it up royally." Tori gave me a questioning look. "I let him go."

"What do you mean you let him go? Did you tell him about the baby?" Tori went and sat on the edge of her bed across from mine.

I sat up and leaned against the headboard. "He doesn't want a baby."

"He said he doesn't want his baby?" Anger flashed in Tori's eyes. "What the fuck?"

I lowered my eyes and wrung my hands in my lap, twisting my ring around and around. "That's not what I said." I let out a long sigh. "We were talking hypotheticals. He made it clear that a baby was not part of the plan. Said it would be a disaster." I looked back at Tori. "I didn't tell him."

"Kyla…"

I held my hand up. "Just stop. I couldn't do it. He's got big plans, and they don't include a crying baby that consumes all our time. I set him free. Told him we could be friends." A tear fell down my face. "I ended everything and destroyed both of us in the process."

Tori looked so confused. "If he doesn't know about the baby, why does he think you broke up with him? When I talked to you earlier, it sounded like everything was going so well."

"It was. I was willing to let the other night go. I was willing to forgive it all and move forward. Then we went to dinner and Madison showed up."

"Madison? Who's Madison?" I gave Tori a pointed to look. "Oh shit! Is she…?"

"Yep! She made a big show of thanking Tyler for the other night. Told him he was amazing. Isn't that nice?" I rolled my eyes.

"What did you do?"

"Tori, she was gorgeous. Like really gorgeous. At first, I was mad. I told Tyler I wanted to go home and stormed out of the restaurant. Then, I realized Madison was just trying to get under my skin and she did." I paused and dropped my head.

"And?" Tori urged me to continue.

"But then as I thought about it, I realized this was what I needed to put space between us. I had to do it if he doesn't want a baby. Because this baby is non-negotiable." I rubbed my belly again. "I accused him of Madison being my replacement when I wasn't around. I told him we needed to explore other options. Told him we could still be friends. I was really mean to him. I needed him to be mad at me."

Tori came over and sat next to me. "What happened next?"

"Mission accomplished. He called me a bitch and basically told me to fuck off. I've never seen him so mad or hurt. He dropped me off and left without a word."

Tori wrapped her arms around my shoulders and pulled me into a hug. "This isn't what you wanted is it?"

I shook my head and tears fell from my eyes. "I already miss him." I sniffed. "I don't know if I can do this on my own. What have I done?"

Chapter 14
Tyler

I awoke to the sound of glass clattering. I squinted my eyes and saw Cody picking up beer bottles and putting them in a trash can. "What time is it?" My head throbbed, and my chest hurt.

"It's two in the afternoon. Rough night?"

"You could say that." I let out an exasperated sigh. Cody grabbed a broom and dustpan and started sweeping up the shattered glass from the floor. "I'll get that." I started to get off the bed.

"Dude, I got it. You don't have shoes on." He swept the glass into the dustpan and dumped it in the garbage can. "I take it things didn't go well with Kyla?"

I rubbed at my eyes and ran my hands through my hair. "Actually, everything was going really good. I mean *reeeally* good. I had her back... until last night."

"What happened?"

"Fucking Madison happened. That chick is fucking crazy." I shook my head, remembering the whole scene. "Kyla and I were out having dinner, and I was about to pop the question when Madison showed up. She walked over to us and thanked me for the other night. Fucking thanked me, like it meant something. Like it wasn't the first time. Like we knew each other!" I tried to reel in my anger.

Cody looked up from sweeping. "Oh fuck!"

"Yeah... oh fuck, is right. Kyla blew a fucking gasket. Accused me of cheating, replacing her with Madison. We both said things we shouldn't have. She ended it. Fucking friend-zoned me."

"I'm sorry, man. Maybe you should call her. Talk to her. Three years is a lot to give up on."

"I'm not calling her. She said she needed time." I changed into sweats and a t-shirt and picked up my phone. "Thanks for cleaning up my mess. I'm going to the gym. I need to work off some of this anger and frustration."

My feet pounded on the treadmill. Godsmack blasted in my ears. My mind kept returning to the last couple of days. What a fucking mess! I knew I screwed up, but I really thought we had gotten past that. There had to be something else. I just couldn't figure out what it was.

Was she interested in someone else? She was so up and down, like she was warring with something. Was this about not wanting to have a baby now? That was ridiculous. She knew I wanted to finish college first, get my career settled. Shit, that's what she should want too. We didn't have time for a baby. That couldn't be it. There had to be something else. But what?

It was like she was purposely trying to piss me off. But why? It just didn't make sense. She kept saying she loved me, but did she? I never doubted her before. There had to be someone else. It was the only thing that made sense. Her words replayed in my head. *Maybe you need to explore other options. How do we know we were made for each other when we've never looked beyond each other?* I didn't need to explore other options to know she was the one. I couldn't believe she was gone.

Chapter 15
Kyla

It had been a week. A long, miserable week. I couldn't remember a time when Tyler and I went twenty-four hours without texting or talking. Now it had been a week. God, I missed him. Every day my heart broke a little bit more. I didn't even know that was possible.

My new classes were fine. At least it gave me something else to think about. I was exhausted during the day, but barely slept at night. I wasn't eating like I should. I skipped meals without realizing it. Despite this fact, my morning sickness was in full effect. Every morning, like clockwork, I found myself draped over the toilet, throwing up whatever I had managed to eat.

I was almost eight weeks along and I knew I needed to see a doctor. I was scared. What was I thinking? I couldn't do this by myself.

Tori was studying at her desk, something I rarely saw her do. I think she was hanging out in our room more just to keep an eye on me.

"Tori?" She turned to me as she stuffed a potato chip in her mouth. "I need to ask for a big favor."

"What's that?" she said, chasing her chips with a gulp of Coke.

I was nervous about this because I knew she was disappointed in my decision not to tell Tyler about the baby. "If I made a doctor appointment, would you go with me?"

Tori put down her pen and sighed. "You're still not going to tell Tyler, are you?"

I shook my head. "I can't."

She corrected me. "You can, but you won't. You know how I feel about this. I grew up without my dad. I never even knew who he was. You can't deny Tyler the opportunity to know and make his own decision. He deserves to know, Kyla."

I turned away from her. "Forget it. I'll do it on my own." I had pushed away Ty and now I was pushing away Tori. What was wrong with me?

Tori ran her hand over her face. "I'll go with you. I don't agree with you, but you're not going to do this alone. You're like my sister. I'm not going to abandon you. Are you going to tell your parents?"

"I won't really have a choice, but not yet. They're going to be disappointed in me for not being smarter than this." I stood and gave Tori a hug. "Thank you." I kissed her on the forehead. "Now quit babysitting me and go see Chris."

Tori gave me a surprised look. "How did you know?"

"Seriously? It's Saturday night and you're here studying. I know you get decent grades, but you don't study on Saturday nights. Go have some fun."

Tori grabbed her purse off her desk. "Are you sure?"

I waved her off. "Yes, I'm sure. I'll be fine."

I made my appointment with Dr. Imitra for the following week. Tori and I sat in the waiting room, and I started bouncing my knee. I looked around at all the baby magazines and picked one up. Scanning through it, I quickly put it back down. All of this was getting a little too real for me.

Tori reached over and took my hand. "Are you alright? You look a little pale."

"Honestly? I'm nervous as hell. I'm not ready for this. Maybe we should come back another day." I started to get up from my chair.

Tori put her hand on my shoulder and pushed me back down. "Kyla, you're one of the strongest people I know. You can do this. I'm here for you. You're not alone."

Just then, my name was called. I walked toward the smiling nurse, Tori right behind me. She led us into an exam room where she instructed me to get undressed from the waist down and wait for the doctor. I did as she asked, covered myself with the lightweight blanket and sat up on the table. I glanced at Tori. "I'm scared," I admitted.

Tori moved her chair next to the exam table and reached up to hold my hand. "It's going to be okay. I'm here with you and for you." She gave my hand a little squeeze. I was thankful that Tori was with me, but I still wished it was Tyler holding my hand, telling me everything would be all right.

A light knock came at the door and kind-faced woman walked in and smiled at me. "Hi Kyla. I'm Dr. Imitra, but you can call me Claudia." She extended her hand forward. I took it, giving her a tentative handshake and a nervous smile. "You look scared to death," she said in a gentle tone. "Don't worry. I'm going to take good care of you. So... it looks like you're pregnant," she said looking down at the chart in her hand.

"Yes," I said, not elaborating.

"How far along do you think you are?" she asked.

"I think about nine weeks," I answered.

She nodded her head. "I'm going to assume, from how nervous you are, that this was not planned."

Tears welled in my eyes. "No, it wasn't planned, but I want this baby." I bit my lip, as I tried to keep my emotions at bay. "This is my friend, Tori. She's helping me through this."

Claudia shook hands with Tori and then returned her focus to me. She put her hand on my shoulder. "I know this all seems very scary, but I assure you, I'll be here to help you every step of the way."

I let out a long breath. "Thank you."

"Let's see what's going on. First, I'll do a pelvic exam and then we'll do an ultrasound to see how far along you are. Just lay back and relax."

I did as she asked, placing my feet in the stirrups. Claudia conducted her exam. Her hands were gentle and unobtrusive.

"Okay, you can put your legs down," she said. "Now, let's see if we can get a picture of this little peanut." She pulled the blanket down off my waist a little bit, so that my stomach showed. "This will be a little cold," Claudia said, as she spread a clear gel across my stomach. "I'm just going to rub this wand across your stomach and hopefully we'll get to see your baby."

"See my baby?" I asked in surprise.

"Yep." She smiled at me. "Let's have a look." She dimmed the lights, moved the wand slowly across my stomach and then stopped. I looked at the screen but had no idea what I was looking at.

"There he or she is."

I looked, but still couldn't see anything meaningful. "I don't know what I'm looking for."

Claudia pointed to the screen. "Right here," she said, pointing to a tiny image on the screen. "And this pulsing spot is your baby's heartbeat."

My eyes went wide. "Oh my God. It's so tiny."

Claudia let out a little laugh. "Not for long. He or she is going to start growing pretty fast. By your next appointment we should be able to see more. Then around 18 weeks, we can try to see if it's a boy or a girl. Do you want to hear the heartbeat?"

I couldn't help the smile that spread across my face. "Yes," I said without hesitation.

Claudia flipped a switch on the machine and a whooshing sound filled the room. It was the most beautiful sound I had ever heard. "Can I record it?" I asked.

Claudia smiled down at me, "Of course you can. It's your baby."

Tori went in my purse and pulled out my phone. I found the video app and aimed it at the screen. I recorded for a full minute before pressing stop. A smile spread across my face.

"I'll print out this picture for you and then take some measurements. We can find out exactly how far along you are." Claudia moved the curser over the screen and pressed some buttons. "It looks like you're about ten weeks along. So that will make your due date in early August. A summer baby."

"Thank you, Claudia. Thank you for being so kind to me. I'm still scared, but you're helping me to feel better about this."

"You're welcome, Kyla. I love my job and I'll be here for you until your delivery." She printed the picture and handed it to me. "Can I ask you a personal question, Kyla?"

I nodded my head.

"Was this consensual?" I nodded again. "Have you told the father?" I shook my head. "I didn't think so. You might want to reconsider. You're going to need his support, but I won't pressure you about it. This is your decision."

"I'll think about it. It's complicated," I said, not meeting her eyes.

"It often is. Well, in any case, I want to see you in a month. I'm going to give you some prenatal vitamins. Everything looks good and the baby looks healthy. I don't anticipate any problems. Have you had any morning sickness?"

"Yes. Every morning like clockwork."

"That's normal. It should start to decrease in a couple of weeks when you move into your second trimester. If it gets too bad, let me know." She wiped the gel from my stomach. "Try to eat healthy and stay away from too much caffeine. I'll see you in a month."

Claudia left the room, leaving Tori and me alone. "That was pretty amazing," I said as I was getting dressed.

Tori smiled at me. "Yeah, it was. Tyler would have loved it."

Chapter 16
Tyler

The last few weeks sucked. I hadn't heard from Kyla at all. I almost called her a dozen different times, but I didn't. She wanted the space. I'd tried to respect that, but it was killing me. I filled my days with going to class and working out at the gym.

Tomorrow was my twenty-first birthday. I hadn't spent a birthday without Kyla in three years. It was going to suck, but being legal meant I could legally drown my sorrows.

I had stuck the pictures of Kyla in my desk drawer, along with the engagement ring I bought her. I opened the drawer and pulled out her picture. "Don't go down that road again," Cody said as he walked out of the bathroom from taking his shower.

"I know," I said as I put the picture away. "I just don't get it. Why has she not called? Not texted?"

"I don't know, man. But you haven't exactly reached out to her either."

I sighed. "I know. I just… fuck! I don't know!"

"Dude, it's over. The sooner you accept that, the sooner you can move on. Tomorrow's your birthday. Come out to the club. I'm sure you can find some chick to make you forget all about her."

"I don't know… kind of feels like cheating," I said.

"It's not cheating. She's made it pretty damn clear that it's over. You're just the last one to realize it," Cody pointed out.

"It is fucking over, isn't it?" I said, with more strength in my voice than I'd felt in a long time. "Let's do it! Tomorrow night, I'm taking my life back."

The bass thumped all around me and bodies moved on the dance floor without a care in the world. I walked up to the bar and ordered a Jack and Coke. I didn't usually go for the hard stuff, but I needed a boost to start the night.

All I could think about was the text I got from Kyla this morning.

Ky: Happy Birthday! I miss you!

I didn't know how to respond to that, so I just texted back,

Ty: Thank You!

It was fucking lame. She had finally made some sort of contact with me, and all I could say was thank you.

I should have called her. But I didn't.

I should have told her I missed her too. But I didn't.

I was an idiot!

Cody came up behind me and clamped his hand on my shoulder. "Look around, dude. This place is your playground. Any one of these chicks would fucking come just from being with the quarterback of the Spartans."

"Yeah, well, I'm not very good at this. I've been with Kyla so long…" I couldn't even finish the thought as she crept into my memory.

"Who? I don't even want to hear that name tonight. You're a free agent, man. Go get yourself some." Cody gave me a little push forward. "Get up in there."

I downed my Jack and Coke and ordered another. I was going to need the liquid courage to make a move. I drank it in a few gulps and moved to the dance floor where a ton of girls were dancing. I stepped up behind one girl, grabbed her by the hips, and started moving to the beat with her. I leaned my head forward and nuzzled her between the neck and shoulder. She turned her head and looked at me.

Fucking Madison!

You've got to be kidding me! I pulled my hands away, like I had been burned and took a step back. "Oh, hell no!"

I turned around and headed back to the bar. I didn't need that kind of aggravation tonight. I felt her grab my arm. I turned and gave her a death glare.

She looked up at me. "You're starting to make it a habit of coming on to me and then walking away."

"I'm not coming on to you. It was a mistake."

"Like the night you fucked me?" She smirked at me.

A growl came up from deep in my chest. "Exactly!" I shook her hand off me and continued toward the bar.

"Listen, I'm sorry!" she yelled above the music. She took me by the arm again. "Buy me a drink and let's talk about it. You and me"

"There's not a you and me. Never was, never will be."

"One drink. That's all I'm asking for. Then we can go our separate ways." God, this girl was persistent.

"Fine. One drink." I walked ahead of her to the bar and sat down on an empty chair. Madison sidled up next to me. We order our drinks, and I scooted my chair away from Madison's to put some space between us.

"I don't bite," she said, taking a sip of her drink.

"That's a matter of opinion. Seems like every time I get close to you, bad shit happens." I took a long swig of my beer. No more liquor for me. I needed to keep a clear head around this chick. "So, talk."

"What happened with you and your girl?" she asked.

"You should know, since you're responsible for crashing that train," I said through gritted teeth. I kept my focus on the bottles behind the bar. I didn't even want to look at her.

"Oh, so that's all my fault? You gonna take any responsibility, superstar?"

I turned to face Madison, giving her a look of disgust. "I took responsibility with my girl. We had things worked out, and then you showed up at the restaurant and put on quite the little show for her. Fucking thanks a lot!"

"She must be something special if she was willing to take you back."

"Yeah, she was. I mean... she is. What the fuck were you thinking, saying that shit at the restaurant? You acted like we," I pointed back and forth between the two of us, "were a couple. You knew what happened at that party was nothing."

"Was it? Nothing, I mean? You seemed pretty into me at the time. Besides, I wanted to see if you and... what's her name... were still together."

I was getting more pissed by the second. "Her name is Kyla. And yeah, we were still together."

Madison quirked her eyebrow at me. "And you're not anymore?"

I threw my hands up. "Fuck if I know! I guess we're on a break."

Madison hopped down off her chair and set her empty glass on the bar. "Well, when you figure it out, let me know. My offer still stands." She walked back toward the dance floor and disappeared into the crowd.

That fucking chick was trouble. Of all the girls I could have grabbed that night, why did it have to be that crazy bitch?

I stayed at the bar for the rest of the night. I didn't want to dance with anyone else. It felt wrong. I should have called Kyla when she texted me this morning. She said she missed me. That was a good sign, right? I missed her, too. As much as I should have admitted that it was over between the two of us, I couldn't. It might have sounded easy to move on, but it wasn't.

I had two more beers and took a cab home. This birthday, which should have been great, pretty much sucked.

Chapter 17
Kyla

I had my second appointment with Dr. Imitra this week. She did another ultrasound and assured me that everything was progressing normally. I took the picture she printed out for me and put it in my purple box of memories, which now sat permanently on top of my desk, instead of in the closet. The picture clearly showed the outline of our baby, it didn't look like a tiny peanut anymore. I could make out his or her teeny arms and legs. Dr. Imitra said we would probably be able to tell if it was a boy or girl at my next visit.

My morning sickness had subsided, like she said it would. I was relieved about that, because throwing up every morning was miserable. My belly was beginning to show a small baby bump. I was thankful for the cold weather, because it meant I could wear sweatshirts, and no one would question. I wasn't ready for anyone, except Tori, to know I was pregnant.

After a long talk with Dr. Imitra, or Claudia as she preferred, I decided to tell Tyler about our baby. Tori, although she hadn't been riding me about it, said it was about time. I was nervous about my decision, but I really wanted to share this with him. If he was mad about the baby, so be it. But it was a chance I needed to take. Hopefully, he would tell me he wanted to be part of our lives. Hopefully, we could go back to being us. Hopefully, he would understand why I felt the need to hide this from him. Hopefully.

I sat on my bed and picked up my phone. My finger hovered over his number, and I pressed send before I could change my mind. It rang three times before he picked up. My heart was beating out of my chest as I ran my finger over the scar on my knee. Something I did when I was nervous.

"Hello," he said, like he didn't know who it was.

"Hi, Ty," I said hesitantly.

"Kyla, I didn't expect to hear from you."

"I know. I've been stupid. Do you have time to talk?" *Please say yes.*

"Yeah. I just left my last class for the day. What's up?" He sounded detached. His guard was up, and I couldn't blame him.

I took a deep breath. "I need to tell you that I'm sorry. I've been selfish, and I said a lot of things I didn't mean."

He sighed on the other end of the line. "We both did," he admitted. "I'm sorry, too."

I was starting to get emotional, and my voice caught in my throat. "I miss you so much," I choked back a sob, as a tear ran down my cheek.

Tyler's voice softened. "I fucking miss you too, baby."

I closed my eyes as more tears ran down my cheeks. "Do you think we can fix this? Fix us? Would you be willing to try?" He didn't answer, and I started to ramble. "If not, I get it. I know this was my doing and you've probably moved on, but I just thought maybe we could try. And I…"

"Ky, stop talking. I love you. I want to try. I've missed you like crazy."

I let out the breath I'd been holding. "I love you too. I don't know how to do this without you," I admitted. "I feel like I've not just lost my boyfriend, but my best friend."

"Are you still wearing my ring?"

I looked down at my hand where Tyler's ring sat. "Yes. I've never taken it off."

"Remember what I told you. It's my heart. You still have it."

I tried to cover the phone as I sniffed back my tears that freely flowed down my face. I hadn't realized this was going to be so hard. "I remember." He hadn't completely given up on us.

"Don't cry, baby. We can fix this. I just need to know why you ran. I told you, don't run away, talk to me."

"I know, but it's not something I could talk to you about then. Can you come see me? I promise I'll explain everything. I need to do this face to face, not over the phone."

"I can come tomorrow after class. My last class ends at four. Should I pack a bag?" he asked.

I wasn't sure he would want to stay after I told him about our baby, but I told him the truth. "Yes. I want you to stay."

The next day, I was both excited and nervous. I was excited to see Tyler after almost six weeks of being apart. I was nervous because I didn't know how he was going to react to me being pregnant. I was going to show him the ultrasound pictures and let him watch the video I made of the baby's heartbeat. After seeing that, he would have to fall in love with our baby. Just like I did. Right?

I looked at my phone. I had a while until he got here, so I threw on a tank top and shorts while I started to get ready. I would change later.

I started doing my makeup when I felt a cramp in my stomach. I put my hand over my tiny baby bump and rubbed it. It went away, and I started to put my eyeshadow on. I had just finished my eyeliner when another cramp hit me low in my abdomen and I doubled over in pain. "What the hell?" I leaned against the bathroom wall for support. The third cramp came fast. I felt like I was being stabbed in the stomach. The pain was unbearable. I felt woozy and I broke out in a cold sweat. Sliding down the wall, I sat on the floor. Something was not right. Something was wrong with the baby. I knew it.

I looked between my legs. Blood ran down the insides of my thighs. I tried to get up to reach my phone that was on my desk. I needed to call Tori. I needed help.

Another cramp, worse than the others ripped through me. I fell back to the floor. The cool tile felt good on my face. My vision started to spot, and I fought to stay conscious. Blood smeared across the bathroom floor, as I crawled toward the door. There was so much blood. I wasn't going to make it to my phone. I was losing my baby. And I hadn't even told Ty yet.

I heard the door open. Then Tori and Chris's voices floated into the room. "Kyla, I hope you're decent. Chris is here."

My voice came out weak and strained. "Tori!"

I saw her feet in front me. "Oh my God, Kyla!"

"Something's wrong with the baby. I need to go to the hospital."

Tori reached down to try and pick me up, but I was dead weight. She was down on the ground with me when she yelled, "Chris, get in here! Now!"

Chris came around the corner. "What the fuck? Where is all that blood coming from?"

Tori looked up at him. "She's miscarrying. We need to get her to the hospital."

Chris was shocked. "She's pregnant?"

Tori got impatient. "Yes, I need you to help me pick her up."

"Screw that!" He tossed Tori his keys. "Go get my truck and pull it up front. I got her."

Tori rushed out of the room. Chris grabbed a blanket and scooped me up in his arms. I tried to keep my head up, but it felt so heavy. "Don't you pass out on me, baby girl. You gotta stay with me. You hear me?"

I nodded my head and then everything went black.

Chapter 18
Tyler

I had just gotten on the road to go see Kyla. I was so happy when had she called. Surprised, but happy. She had missed me as much as I missed her. And that fact, made me secretly satisfied. I knew we could work this out, although I still needed to know why she ran. I thought it was about Madison, but maybe it wasn't.

My phone sitting in the cup holder buzzed. I picked it up and saw it was Chris. "Hey, Chris. Long time, no talk. What's up, man?"

"Tyler, you need to come out here right now." His voice was serious, not even a bit of humor in his usually easy-going voice.

"I'm already on my way. Kyla called yesterday. We're going to try and fix this shit between us. I should be at the dorms in a little over an hour. What's going on?"

I could hear Chris take a deep breath on the other side of the line. "Don't go to the dorms. You need to come to the hospital."

Fear gripped me, and I quickly pulled over on the shoulder. "What the fuck is going on? Is Kyla okay?"

"Honestly, I don't know. She scared the fuck out of us. Tori and I came back to her room, and Kyla was laying on the bathroom floor. There was fucking blood everywhere." I heard him sigh and then his voice got really quiet. "Tori thinks she's having a miscarriage."

Shock ripped through my body. I was frozen as his words sunk in. The words that came next, came out disjointed. "A… miscarriage? She's… pregnant?"

"Apparently. I didn't know. And from the tone of your voice, I'm assuming you didn't either."

I don't know why the next thought even crossed my mind, I guess I was in shock. I stuttered, "Is it... is it mine?"

I heard an exasperated sigh. "Yeah fucker... I'm pretty sure it's yours. She hasn't been with anyone else. She barely leaves her room, except to go to class. Just... just get here. She passed out on me when I carried her out to my truck. She didn't look good, and nobody has told us anything yet."

I pulled my shit together and pulled up my GPS. "Which hospital are you at?"

"Bronson Methodist Hospital. We're waiting in the ER."

I punched it into the GPS. "Okay, I got it. I'll be there as soon as I can." I hung up and pulled back onto the road. My mind started spinning. She was pregnant? With our baby? Why didn't she tell me? How was that possible? We only had unprotected sex that one time at Christmas and I pulled out. Fuck!

I pulled up at the ER in record time and rushed inside. Tori and Chris were sitting in the far corner talking quietly. When Tori saw me, she flung herself at me, hugging me tight. "Don't be mad. I told her to tell you, but she said she couldn't. She didn't tell anyone. She kept it a secret."

I pulled Tori off me. "How long have you known?" Tears ran down my face, and I wiped them away with the back of my hand.

Tori dropped her hand to her head. "A while, but she swore me to secrecy. It wasn't my secret to tell. I didn't even tell Chris."

Just then a nurse came out into the waiting room. "The family of Kyla O'Malley." We walked over to the nurse. She looked at us skeptically. "I can only talk to her family."

Tori piped up, "She's my sister."

I quickly added, "She's my fiancé."

The nurse gave us a doubtful look. I don't think she believed us. "Kyla is out of surgery. They're just getting her into a room right now. She's going to be fine." The nurse's face turned sympathetic. "She did lose the baby and a lot of blood. We're keeping her overnight for observation, but she should be able to go home tomorrow. It will just be a few more minutes. I'll come get you when you can see her." The nurse walked away, leaving us standing there.

Tori put her hand on my shoulder. "She's going to be okay and that's the important thing." I wiped away another tear and blew out a breath. I was in a daze. I had just found out I was going to be a father and had it ripped away in less than an hour. I really didn't know what to feel. I was kind of numb to be honest.

The nurse had said a few minutes, but it seemed like we waited forever. I sat in the waiting room bouncing my knee up and down, trying to process everything. Finally, the nurse came back and said only one of us could see her at a time right now. Tori and I looked at each other. "You go," she said. "She was planning on telling you tonight. That's why she asked you to come."

I nodded and followed the nurse. "She's still a little bit out of it. The anesthesia is still wearing off. And... I'm sorry for your loss." She looked at me with sympathy.

I was still processing. The loss hadn't registered yet. The only thing that registered was that my girl was lying in a hospital room and that I needed to see her.

I walked into the room. Kyla looked so tiny in that big bed. She had an IV in her arm, but other than that, she looked like she was sleeping. I pulled the chair next to her bed, sat down, and held her hand. I rubbed my thumb over her delicate fingers. I was getting choked up seeing her like this, but she would be okay. Tears welled in my eyes. The nurse had assured us, that she would be fine.

After a while, her eyes fluttered open, and she drowsily looked over at me. "Hey, baby. How do you feel?"

Her voice was raspy. "Sore." Her other hand went to her stomach and rubbed in small circles. "Is the baby…?"

I shook my head. "I'm sorry." She dropped her head into her hand and started crying. I stood up, pushed her hair back and kissed her forehead "You should have told me. I would have been there for you. I love you." A tear fell down my face and I quickly wiped it away again.

She wiped her tears with the back of her hand. I sat back down in the chair. A million questions came to mind, but I kept them to myself. I held her hand in both of mine, waiting for her to say something. She finally pulled herself together.

"I wanted to tell you, but then all that stuff happened at the party, and there was so much tension between us. I didn't know how to tell you. You didn't want a baby."

I let out a sigh and shook my head. I started making mental calculations. "When did this happen? Was it that time right after Christmas when we didn't use a condom? How would you have even known that quickly?"

She bit her lip and shook her head. A worried look took over her face. "Don't be mad, okay?"

"It was mine, wasn't it? Please tell me it was mine."

She narrowed her eyes at me and pulled her hand away. "Yes, it was yours. I haven't been with anyone else."

I reached over and took her hand back. "I'm sorry. I had to ask. I'm just trying to figure this all out. We always used a condom, except that one time."

"I know, but it just happened. I don't know how, but it did. Something must have leaked or broke. God, I don't know. I didn't plan on this happening either."

"If not then, when? How long have you known?"

"Please don't be mad," she pleaded.

I tried to keep the rising anger out of my voice. "How long, Kyla? How far along were you?"

She winced, "Fourteen weeks. I found out the beginning of December."

I dropped her hand and ran my hands through my hair. "Jesus Christ, Kyla!"

"I'm sorry! I'm sorry I didn't tell you!"

I took a deep breath and ran my hand through my hair again in frustration. "God, it all makes sense now. The throwing up, the not drinking coffee or Coke, your boobs getting bigger. I thought the emotional ups and downs had to do with Madison, but there was more to it. I knew it. I knew there was something else. I just couldn't figure it out." The tears were running down Kyla's cheeks. I took her hand back in mine. "Explain this to me. Explain to me why you didn't tell me."

Kyla bit her lip again. "First of all, I was scared. When I took the test, I panicked. But I knew I was keeping it. Whether we planned it or not, I wanted our baby." She stopped, and I gave her a look that told her to go on. "I knew you didn't want a baby and I didn't know how you were going to react. Then you guys made it to the Rose Bowl, and I couldn't tell you before the game. I didn't want you to be thinking about a baby when you needed to focus on the game."

Understanding started to flicker in my brain. "That's why you didn't want to use a condom before the game. You already knew you were pregnant."

She nodded. "I just wanted to feel closer to you. I was afraid of losing you."

I pinched the bridge of my nose. "So, you didn't tell me because you thought it would mess up my game?"

"It was important. I knew all eyes were going to be on you, including scouts. I didn't want to ruin that for you. And I was afraid of losing you."

"Baby, your more important than football. So, you didn't tell anyone? You carried this around by yourself?"

She nodded again. "I wanted to tell you before anyone else. I was going to tell you the day after the big party. But then shit happened. I was heartbroken. I thought I lost you. That you didn't want to be with me anymore. That's when I told Tori."

"Fuck!" I stood up and started pacing back and forth. "I wish I could just make that night go away. But it's going to haunt me forever, isn't it?"

"Tyler, relax! It's over." She looked at me, a hint of insecurity in her eyes. "It is over, isn't it?"

"Ky, it was just that one time. I promise. There never was or will be anything between Madison and me."

Kyla winced. "I believe you, but can you not say her name? Can we just call her she-who-must-not-be-named? You know, like in Harry Potter?"

I smirked at her. "Yeah, I think we can do that." I sat back down and took her hand again.

"Anyway, then we had that conversation about having kids." She looked down at our joined hands. "You made it pretty clear that you weren't ready. I wasn't going to put this on you if you didn't want it. That's when I knew I had to leave you. I said all the things I said because it was easier if you were mad at me. I tried to push you away. Make you not want me anymore."

"Ky, you ripped my heart out. I would have been there for you. We could have done this together."

Her green eyes pierced mine. "Really? Because I think the words you used were, 'It would be a disaster'. How else was I supposed to read into that?"

I dropped my head, "You're right. I didn't make it any easier for you." I looked back up at her, "But you still should have told me."

A soft knock came at the door and a woman dressed in a lab coat walked in. "Hi, Kyla."

Kyla looked at her and tears welled in her eyes again. "Hi, Dr. Imitra. This is Tyler," she said pointing at me.

Dr. Imitra reached across to shake my hand. "It's good to finally meet you. I've heard a lot about you."

I shook her hand. "I wish I could say the same. This is all... a lot to take in."

Dr. Imitra had kind eyes and a sympathetic tone. "I'm sure it is." She turned back to Kyla. "It was a placental abruption. It wouldn't have shown on the ultrasound."

"I don't understand. You said everything looked normal. Healthy."

Dr. Imitra took Kyla's other hand. "These things just happen. There's nothing you could have done to prevent it. The good news is that we were able to stop the bleeding pretty fast and you should heal normally. So, in the future, when you want to have another baby, getting pregnant shouldn't be an issue. In the meantime, I'm going to prescribe you some birth control pills. I'll check back on you in the morning, but you should be able to go home tomorrow. I'm sorry this happened." Dr. Imitra left as quietly as she had entered.

I focused back on Kyla. "You should have told me. We're not done talking about this." I stood up abruptly, "I need some air. I'll be back." I pushed past Tori as she was headed into the room.

I walked through the waiting room and headed outside. Chris followed me out. I pounded my fist against the wall. "What the fuck!" I turned back around and leaned against the wall.

"You okay, man?"

"Yeah... no. Fuck, I don't know. She should have told me! This is not the way I should have found out! I missed everything! The doctor appointments. The ultrasounds. I wanted to marry her. Did I ever tell you that?" Chris just shook his head. "Yeah, bought a ring and everything. I would have been there for her. She didn't trust me enough to step up to the plate."

"Tori said she's been bugging Kyla about it since she found out. Tori never said a word to me. I kind of freaked out finding her in the bathroom like that."

"Thanks for taking care of her tonight, but it should have been me. I should have been there. She should have told me."

"Tori said Kyla was going to tell you tonight."

"It's a little fucking late, now. God, I wish I smoked because I could really go for a cigarette right now. Or a shot of whisky. Or ten."

Chapter 19
Kyla

Tori came and sat in the chair Tyler just abandoned. "You scared the fuck out of me, girl!"

I gave her a weak smile. "Yeah, I know. Scared myself too. I'm sorry."

"Don't you dare apologize." Tori took ahold of my hand. "I'm just glad you're okay. I'm sorry about the baby. I know you really wanted it."

"I didn't just want it. I loved it. I loved that it was a part of Tyler and me. The best part." Another piece of my heart broke off and shattered on the floor, as I began to come to terms with the reality that I had lost my baby. Our baby. The baby I was scared to death of but had come to love.

"So, how's Tyler taking it?" Tori asked.

"I honestly don't know. It's a lot to take in. He got really pissed after Dr. Imitra left. I think he went to cool off," I said.

"Give him time. Like you said, it's a lot to take in. He'll come around," Tori assured me.

"Yeah, I don't know. Time is the one thing we never have enough of. He'll go back to MSU, and I'll be here. It's easier to be detached when we don't see each other every day. I may have lost him for good this time." Tori gave me a sad look. "It's my own fault. I have no one to blame but myself. You warned me."

"He still loves you or he wouldn't be here," Tori pointed out.

I leaned my head back on the pillow and closed my eyes. "Sometimes love isn't enough."

"You're depressing me. We've been a foursome for a long time. It won't be the same."

"If things don't work out, you can still be friends with Tyler. You don't have to choose one or the other. I wouldn't make you do that."

"I know you wouldn't. But you know my loyalties are with you. You're my sister. That's the only way they would let me back here with you, so it's official now."

I let out a little laugh. "You told them you were my sister? I love you, you know that?"

Tori leaned forward and gave me a tight hug. "I love you too, sister." She let me go and sat back down. "Now we need to talk about something really important… your parents. They are going to get a bill for this you know. And unless you plan on telling them, which I assume you don't, we need to come up with a cover story."

"I hadn't really thought about that yet, but you're right. What did you have in mind? I know you've already thought about this."

"Okay, this is the plan. We'll tell them that you had an ovarian cyst. That way if OB GYN shows up on the paperwork, it won't look suspicious. But you need to call them and assure them that you're fine and they don't need to come out here."

I loved the way Tori's mind worked. "You're brilliant, you know that? Will you stay here while I call them?"

"Of course. I wouldn't let you do this on your own," she said.

"I don't have my phone. Can I use yours?"

"Yeah, of course." She pulled out her phone and handed it to me.

I punched in their number. "Here goes nothing." I waited as it rang, and my mom picked up. "Hi, Mom…"

Thankfully, my mom bought the story... hook, line, and sinker. I convinced her it was no big deal, and they didn't have to come out. I promised I would call them the next day.

I was just hanging up with my mom when Tyler walked back in.

"Okay, Mom, I'll talk to you later. Don't worry, everything is under control. Yes, I'm fine. I'll talk to you tomorrow."

Tori got up and excused herself when Tyler came back in. I got nervous again, knowing how upset Ty had been. "Hey," I said, not knowing what else to say.

"Got that lying thing down to a science, don't you?" Tyler sat down in the seat Tori just abandoned. He leaned back in the chair, putting distance between us. His eyes were focused and angry. I looked away because I just couldn't take it. The disappointment. The anger.

"I did what I had to do," I stated plainly, like there was no other option. "Just like I did with us. You weren't ready for this. I did what I had to do."

"Bullshit! You had choices! You chose not to tell me! You didn't trust me!" His anger was evident. "You should have told me. I missed everything. I didn't get to be there for the doctor's appointments. The ultrasounds. Nothing. I missed everything. I just get to be here as the clean-up crew. Picking up the pieces of what once was."

I was pissed. "You think I planned this? Why do you think I asked you to come see me tonight? I was going to tell you! I didn't know whether you'd stay or leave me. I didn't want to lose our baby. I loved our baby! Maybe you can't understand that because you never wanted it to begin with. But... fuck... just leave... you don't understand." The tears ran down my face. "I trusted you and you betrayed me with what's-her-face!" I wished I could run away, but I was harnessed by this stupid IV. I reached over and ripped the IV from my arm. I just wanted to go home. Blood trickled down my arm, but I didn't care.

"What the fuck are you doing?" Tyler's eyes went big.

"I'm fucking done! While you were off fucking someone else, I was carrying your baby. You don't get it." I climbed out of the bed and started searching for my clothes. I found the bag and started crying. "Fucking great! Everything is covered in blood!"

"Just stop!" Tyler grabbed my arms and shook me.

"Why? You had nothing invested in this. Just fucking admit it. You're relieved. You're thankful that I miscarried. It would have been a disaster. Remember?" The hate I was feeling spewed from my mouth. Not hate for Tyler, but for the situation. I was so furious. I couldn't think straight.

"Why are you acting like this? I should be the one mad, not you!"

I calmed down. "You're right. You have every reason to be mad." The anger seeped from my body and all that was left was regret. I collapsed to the floor. I was so tired. Tired of lying. Tired of the guilt. Tired of trying to be strong.

Tyler picked me up and put me back on the bed. He took some tissues from the side table and started to clean the blood from my arm. I laid down and turned away from him. I couldn't look at Tyler. It hurt too much.

I stared off, focusing on the dark night outside the window. I needed to be honest with him. It was the least I could do. My voice held no anger anymore, just sadness. "I don't know what happened to us. We were so happy, so in love. Now I have this gaping hole in my chest. Somewhere in all of this we broke, and I don't know how to fix it. I called you because I wanted you to be part of this with me. I thought maybe, just maybe, we could be happy again. I didn't call you to clean up my mess."

I felt the bed dip behind me. Tyler laid next to me and wrapped his arm around my waist. "Just because I'm mad at you, Kyla, doesn't mean I don't love you. I'll always love you."

I turned in his arms to face him. "I'll always love you, too. But it seems like all we do lately is try to destroy each other.

Hurt each other. We never used to talk to one another like we do now. There's so much anger between us."

Tyler ran his fingers through my messy hair. "Maybe you're right. We're broken. I know I hurt you, but you hurt me too. I don't know how to fix us either."

I looked up into his blue eyes. "So, what do we do? How do we go on from here?"

Tyler had tears in his eyes. "We let go. Try to find happiness. And maybe, somewhere down the road, we can try again."

The tears ran down my face. "I don't wanna let go. I don't know how to be without you." Tyler kissed me. It was slow and sensual. We poured everything into that kiss. Our hearts, our souls, our love, our hurt, our anger. It was our goodbye. "Please stay with me tonight. Just one more night."

He pulled me in close. "One more night."

I closed my eyes, and the exhaustion took over. It was the best sleep I'd had in weeks. I felt warm and safe in his arms.

When I woke in the morning, Tyler was gone.

Chapter 20
Tyler

Walking out of that room was the hardest thing I've ever done. I knew if I waited until Kyla woke up, I would never leave. It was better this way.

I had lain next to Kyla until she fell asleep. I watched her sleep for a long time, then I said goodbye to my heart and slipped out of her arms. I didn't leave a note. I just left.

It had been a week since I left her. And the hole in my chest hadn't closed at all. I still thought about her twenty-four seven and almost called her a dozen different times. I knew we needed to make a clean break. This was harder than back in January, because back then, there was a chance that we would get back together. This time it was final.

I took the ring I bought Kyla and all her pictures and shoved them in the back of a drawer. I couldn't look at them anymore. I took the lotion she left on my bathroom counter, along with a hair tie, and shoved them in the back of the drawer too. I had tried to throw them away, and I did, but then I pulled them out of the garbage can and put them in the drawer. Pieces of her were everywhere. Everything I looked at had a memory. This room alone held a ton of memories.

Once the semester was over, I needed to find an apartment. Maybe I could convince Cody to move in with me, so we could split the cost. I decided not to go home for the summer. There was too much of a chance of running into her at home.

On the plus side, I put all my extra time into working out. I would be in excellent condition by the time football started again. Scouts from the NFL had started to contact me, and I was sure my dream of playing professional football was really going to happen. I thought about skipping my senior year, and just going pro, but I could hear my dad in the back of my head. *You need a college education, son. Nothing is a sure thing. What if you get injured? It'll end your career and you'll have nothing to fall back on.* I knew he was right, but damn it was tempting. And it would take me far away from Kyla.

Chapter 21
Kyla

It had been a month, and the hurt hadn't gone away. If anything, it was worse. I lost my best friend, my other half, and my baby all in the same night. I felt empty. I was a shell of myself. I couldn't eat, and I couldn't sleep.

When I did sleep, the nightmares woke me up. They were all versions of the same things. Either Tyler abandoning me somewhere as I begged him to come back, or someone was trying to take my baby from me. In the really awful nightmares, it was Tyler stealing my baby, telling me I didn't deserve her. In my dreams, my baby was always a girl. A chubby little bundle of love with dark hair and blue eyes.

My nightmares got so bad, that I began to wake Tori with my screaming. I would wake drenched in sweat and crying. Tori said I needed to ask Dr. Imitra to prescribe me something to help me sleep. When I went to see her for my follow-up visit, I told Dr. Imitra about my nightmares. She gave me a prescription for Xanax. I could take them during the day if needed, but I mainly took them at night. The sleep they helped provide was heavenly.

My grades were slipping, but I kept them high enough to maintain my scholarship. Barely. I usually made it to class, but was distracted most of the time, drawing in my notebook. I did the minimum on my homework. Luckily, school had never been that difficult for me, so I was still able to pass my tests. My grades this semester weren't what they should have been, but they were enough.

Tori said I was depressed, but I knew the truth. I was brokenhearted. There was no way I could pick up the pieces of my shattered heart and put them back together. The pieces were too jagged to fit together properly. There where gaping holes where pieces of my heart would forever be missing.

I had tried calling Tyler several times. It always went to voicemail. I begged him to come back to me.

He never called.

I tried to text him, but every text went unanswered.

I would lay on my bed for hours with my earbuds in, listening to music on my phone. There was only one song on the playlist. Nickelback's "Far Away" played on repeat over and over in my head. I wanted to believe that Tyler still loved me. I wanted to believe that he missed me as much as I missed him. I couldn't breathe without him. But he was so far away, not just physically, but emotionally. I didn't want to try again *down the road*. I needed him now.

When my birthday came and went without even a text from Tyler, I knew it really was over. I think another little piece of my heart shattered on that day. I thought for sure I would hear from him. But I didn't.

By the time the end of the second month rolled around, Tori had had enough. She ripped the earbuds out of my ears. "This has gone on for too long. When's the last time you even took a shower?"

I thought about it. "Two days ago. I think." Honestly, I wasn't sure.

"Try four," she said. God, had it really been that long? "He's gone, Kyla. He's not coming back. You need to face the truth because what you're doing isn't healthy."

"You don't know he's not coming back!" I shouted at her. "You don't know what you're talking about."

Tori sat on the bed next to me. She was going to have a come-to-Jesus talk with me and I knew I wasn't going to like it. "Yeah, I do. Chris saw him last weekend. They were out at the bar, and he had plenty of girl company. He looked happy. He's moved on."

"He's moved on? He can't. He promised I had his heart," I insisted.

"Yeah, we need to talk about that too." Tori picked up my right hand and I quickly pulled it back.

"I'm not taking it off," I stated definitively.

Tori took my hand back and slipped the purple heart-shaped ring off my finger. "Yes, you are," she said. "You're not wearing this anymore. I'll put it in the box, but it's not going to be on your hand." Tori walked to the closet and slipped the ring inside my memory box. "You need to start moving on too. I suggest you start by taking a shower. No offense, but you're starting to smell."

I pulled my shirt up over my nose and sniffed. Okay, I did smell a little bit. "It's not that bad," I said.

"It's not that great either," she said. "Go shower and get ready. You're going to the bar with us tonight."

"I really don't want to go to the bar," I protested.

"You're going! And you're going to have fun. And you can get shit-faced because Chris is driving. We're having a girls' night, and he'll drive our drunk asses home. Now go."

Jeez, talk about bossy!

⦵♡

We got to the bar a little after eight. It was already crowded, and the music was thumping. The three of us found a table in the corner. I needed to eat first if I was going to drink. I grabbed a menu and started checking out my choices.

Tori pulled the menu from my hand. "You're stalling," she said.

I rolled my eyes at her. "I'm not stalling. I'm hungry. You just finished telling me I needed to eat more. I'm going to eat."

The waitress came over and took our orders. I ordered my food and a diet Coke.

Tori glared at me. "She'll have a Captain and diet Coke. And can we get a round of shots? Tequila."

I gave Tori a dirty look. Chris laughed and shook his head. "You might as we'll give up, Kyla. You know when Tori sets her mind on something, she always gets her way."

"Yeah," I huffed. "I know."

"You're drinking. End of story." Tori got up and walked to the bathroom.

I watched her walk away and then leaned over the table to Chris. "Tori said you saw Tyler last weekend," I said in a low voice.

Chris pushed back from the table. "Oh no! We're not talking about that."

"Please! I just want to know if he's okay," I said. I looked down at my naked hand. "If he's moved on."

Chris let out an exasperated sigh. "I can't believe you're asking me this. Do you really want to know?"

I nodded my head. "Yes. I need to know."

"He's happy, Kyla. I wouldn't normally tell you this, but you're right. You need to know. He went home with somebody. He's moved on."

My face fell. "Oh… well, good for him. I guess."

"You need to do the same. He's not coming back."

I waved him off. "Yeah, I know." Pretending it didn't bother me was hard.

Tori came back to the table. "What are you two talking about?" she asked suspiciously.

"Nothing," I replied. Just then the waitress showed up with our drinks and shots. Before she left, I asked, "Can you bring another round of these when you come back?" She nodded and left. I picked up my tequila. "To moving on," I toasted. I threw the shot back. It tasted awful and burned on the way down. My throat was on fire.

"Damn, girl," Chris said. He pushed his glass of water toward me. "Need a chaser?"

I took a long drink from his glass to help put the fire out. "Thanks." I picked up my Captain and diet Coke and downed half of it. Our food and next round of shots came. I quickly ate my burger and fries. I hadn't realized how hungry I was, and that greasy burger tasted divine. After downing the other half of my drink, I pointed to the shots. "Round two?"

Chris pushed his toward me. "You can have mine too. I'm driving, remember?"

Tori and I picked up our shots. I was starting to feel the effect of the first shot when I raised the glass. "To ex-boyfriends fucking other bitches," I exclaimed. Tori almost choked on her shot when those words came out of my mouth. I downed my tequila and Chris's. The fire in my throat burned. I waved my hand in front of my mouth and scrunched up my face in disgust. I grabbed Chris's glass of water to put the fire out again. Chris just laughed.

"Let's go dance!" I shouted.

"You girls go. I'll order more drinks." Chris was going to let us have our night and I loved him for it.

I grabbed Tori by the hand and led her to the dance floor. It felt like so long since I'd danced and had fun. I shook my hips and waved my hands in the air. Tori and I giggled and danced for several songs. I could really feel the tequila taking effect. I felt good. Loose and free. When the music changed to a slow song, Tori and I started to head back to the table.

"Where are you going, beautiful?" I felt a hand snake around my waist, pulling me back to the dance floor. I looked up into chocolate brown eyes and blond hair. So not Tyler, but he was cute, and I let him lead me back. I wrapped my hands around his neck and swayed with the music. I pretended not to notice that his eyes were brown instead of blue. This was part of moving on. Right?

When the song ended, I thanked him and turned out of his arms. He caught me by the hand. "Buy you a drink?"

I shrugged. "Sure. Why not?"

"What are you drinking?"

"Captain and diet Coke." I followed him to the bar where we found two empty chairs.

He ordered our drinks and turned to me. "What's your name?"

"Kyla."

"I'm Jake. Nice to meet you." He reached over to shake my hand. "So, what's your story?"

"What do you mean?" I asked.

"Well, you're a beautiful girl here without a date. No boyfriend?"

"Wow! Right to the point, huh?" I took a sip of my drink and gave him a flirty smile.

"I'm not into other guy's girls, so it's always the first question I ask."

"That's very honorable of you, Jake. Been burned before?" I questioned.

"Many times. So, what's the story?" he smiled at me, and he had killer dimples that reminded me of Tyler's. I pushed the thought from my head.

"I'm recently single and if we're being honest, I'm not really in the market for a boyfriend." Even if Tyler had moved on, there was no way I was ready to make the leap. Baby steps.

Jake put his hand to his chest. "Oh… you're killing me here. How recently?"

I smiled and took a sip of my drink. "Two months. Less since I've accepted it," I said, keeping it vague.

"Two months isn't too recent. Long term relationship?"

"Three years. We started dating in high school. Things just got complicated." I don't know why I was spilling my past, but the conversation came easy, and I was proud of myself for even being able to talk about it without breaking down. The alcohol was definitely making my inhibitions disappear.

"Does he go to Western?"

"Nah. He goes to State. Plays football there."

"Really?" he asked. "I've got friends on the team. What's his name? Maybe I know him." Wouldn't that be my luck? What would be the chances that I'd be talking to someone Tyler knew. But then again, maybe it would get back to him that I had moved on too. Jealousy was an evil bitch, but she could play in my favor.

I let out a sigh. "Tyler. He's the quarterback."

Jake's eyes lit up with recognition. "Tyler Jackson? That guy's awesome! He's going pro for sure."

I dropped my head to the bar and groaned. "Of all the guys I could have met, you'd have to be a fan of his?"

He laughed. "Sorry, it's just that he's kind of legendary. He was pretty great in the Rose Bowl."

I lifted my head from my arms and looked up at Jake. "Yeah, I know. I was there."

"No shit! I bet that was pretty cool."

"Yeah, it was." I sat back up and took another drink. "No offense, but you're killing my buzz. Now that you know about me, what's your story?"

Jake finished his beer and ordered another. "No story really. Just haven't found the right girl. Plenty of dates, but haven't found 'the one'," he air quoted.

I laughed. "Did you seriously just air quote?" He laughed with me. "Don't mean to burst your bubble, but I'm not sure that I'm ready to date yet. And I'm definitely not ready for a one-night stand."

"Wow! Pretty sure of yourself, aren't you?"

Embarrassment crept up my neck into my cheeks. "I didn't mean…" I stuttered.

"Relax, I'm joking with you! I'd totally date you." I breathed out a sigh of relief. "So, if you won't date me, how about coffee tomorrow? We can just get to know each other."

"Coffee I can do." We exchanged numbers and agreed to meet at the cafe the next day. "Wanna dance again?" I asked.

He flashed that dimpled smile. "Thought you'd never ask."

Chapter 22
Tyler

Kyla had called and texted me, but I never responded. We needed a clean break, and I knew talking to her would just make things harder. I loved her, but I was so mad at her. I needed to move on.

I found an apartment close to campus and moved in before the end of the semester. Cody was going home for the summer but would be moving in next fall. I loved my new place. There were no old memories to haunt me there. It was a fresh start. All part of moving on.

Every weekend I would hit the bar with the guys. I saw Madison a few times. We kept it friendly, but nothing more. I had promised Kyla that there would never be anything between Madison and me. I kept that promise. I owed her that much.

I had no problem picking up girls. They flocked to me like bees to honey. I tried to fuck Kyla out of my brain. I usually drank too much and took some hottie home with me. Brown eyes, blue, hazel… they were all on my list. Never green. I couldn't look at a girl with green eyes and not think of Kyla. I made it clear to the girls that all I was looking for was a one-night stand. I couldn't handle, nor did I want, anything more. They didn't care. They were fine with a down and dirty quick fuck. I was good with that. No complications. No strings. No attachments.

My phone was ringing. I blindly groped around on the nightstand to find it, but it stopped ringing before I could answer it. I looked next to me and saw the dark-haired chick with a banging body from last night. The sheet barely covered her naked body. I poked her in the side. "Time to go home, darling."

My head was throbbing. I got up, threw on some sweats, and went to the kitchen. I grabbed a Gatorade from the fridge and used it to wash down a few Motrin. I went back to the bedroom to kick the chick out of my bed.

I shook her again. "Hey. You gotta go home."

She turned her head and grumbled. "Really? Do you even remember my name?"

"Nope. Doesn't matter. You gotta go."

She huffed, crawled out of bed, and started getting dressed. Damn, she had nice tits. "You're an asshole, you know that?"

"Yep. But you knew that last night and you still fucked me, so that's on you."

She finished gathering her things and headed toward the door. "Even if you are an asshole, it was totally worth it. You fuck like a champ. Call me." She opened the door and left.

I just rolled my eyes. This was too easy.

I went back to my room to check the missed call. My dad. He rarely called. I wondered what he wanted. I called him back and he answered on the first ring. "Hey, Ty. How are things going?"

"Good, Dad. What's up?"

"Well, now that you're not living on campus, I worry about you. I know this thing with you and Kyla hasn't been easy on you."

I groaned. "Can we not talk about her? I'm fine. Everything is great. I'm over it."

I wasn't.

"Good. Good. Glad to hear it."

"Really, I'm fine. The new apartment is great. Thanks for helping me get this place."

"No problem, son. I'm glad to help. But you aren't going to need my help anymore."

What the hell did that mean? "Are you cutting me off? Are you having money problems?" I asked.

"No, no, nothing like that. Your mother and I have plenty of money. You know that. I said that you wouldn't need our help, not that we wouldn't help you."

I was so confused. "I don't know what that means, Dad. You're not making any sense."

"Are you sitting down?" he asked.

"No. What's going on?" I sat down on the edge of my bed. What the hell was he going to tell me?

"Well, you know your grandfather, my dad, had a lot of money, right?"

"Yeah, you and Mom inherited it." That money had paid for my Challenger.

"Not all of it. He left a trust fund for his only grandson. As of your twenty-first birthday, it transferred to you."

I lay back on my bed. "Are you shitting me?"

My dad let out a loud boisterous laugh. "No, I'm not shitting you. It's a lot of money, Tyler."

"How much?" The curiosity was killing me.

"A lot, Tyler."

"Dad, stop dicking me around. How much?"

"Two million." Shock took over my body. Two million dollars? "Tyler, are you still there?"

I shook my head. "Yeah, Dad. Just processing. Is this a joke?"

"Son, you know I don't joke about money. I never told you because I wanted you to learn how to work for what you wanted. I know it sounds like a lot of money, but it can go fast if you're reckless with it."

"Dad, I wouldn't even know where to start."

"Here's my advice. Buy yourself something nice and save the rest. You never know when you might really need it. I can set you up with my financial advisor when you're in town next time."

"I can't believe this. I don't even know what to say."

"You don't have to say anything. I'll send you the account information and Harold's number. You can set up an appointment with him. You're an adult now, so what you do with the money is up to you."

"Thanks, Dad. This is a lot to take in."

"I know. I gotta go, your mother wants me to go to some farmer's market with her." He sighed. "The things we do for the women we love."

Ain't that the truth. "Okay. Give my love to Mom. I'll talk to you soon." I hung up the phone, still in disbelief. Two million dollars? This was crazy!

There were two things I wanted to do with the money, and then I would save the rest. I drove just out of town to the closest Harley dealership. I walked in and started looking around the showroom. A salesman walked over. I could tell he was sizing me up, figuring there was no way I could afford one of these. "Can I help you?"

I was looking at a sleek, black bike. All black and chrome, sexy as hell. I couldn't help but think how good Kyla would look on the back of that thing and what she would look like bent over it. "Yeah. I'm in the market for buying a bike. Tell me about this one here."

The guy gave me skeptical look. "That baby there is very expensive. We have some used bikes over in the other part of the showroom that you might be interested in."

I stuck my hands in my pockets and gave him a pointed look. "I'm not interested in used. I'd like to know about this one."

He let out a sigh, like I was wasting his time. "Yeah, okay." He started telling me all the specs on the bike. I was listening, but this bike was like an orgasm waiting to happen. When he finished talking, I sat on the bike and almost groaned at how it felt between my legs. I fell in love with it.

"I'll take it," I said with authority.

"Well, let's go over to my office and talk about financing. I'm not gonna lie kid, the payments on this thing are going to be hefty."

He started to walk away, but I didn't follow. "I won't be needing financing," I called out to him.

The salesman turned and looked at me questioningly. "Change your mind?"

I shook my head. "Nope. I'll be paying cash. I'll need a jacket and a helmet, too. Think you can help me with that?"

The look on the guy's face was priceless. So, this is what it felt like to have money. I arranged to have the bike delivered to my apartment and walked back to my car with my new jacket and helmet. I had one more stop to make.

A few minutes later, I pulled up in front of the tattoo shop.

Chapter 23
Kyla

Nothing ever happened between Jake and me. We had coffee a few times, and we actually became friends. He told me about his sad love life, and I told him about mine. It was nice to have someone to talk to besides Chris and Tori. Jake knew I was still hung up on Tyler and wasn't ready for anything more than a casual relationship. My heart was still a mangled mess, and it wouldn't be fair to lead Jake into believing otherwise. We went out on a few "friend dates". Jake always held my hand, which felt nice, but he never tried anything else.

The semester was ending in a few days, and I would be going home for the summer. Jake and I promised to keep in touch and went our separate ways.

Chris, Tori, and I all headed home. Chris didn't have much to bring home, but Tori and I filled his truck with all our shit. We stopped at my house first and unloaded all my stuff.

My mom and dad were so happy I was home. I think they missed their baby girl. My mom was concerned about my health. She said I looked too skinny. I had lost a lot of weight, but I was gradually putting it back on. She tried to talk to me about what happened with Tyler. I never told her the truth. I only told her that we grew apart, which was partially true. They didn't need to know about the cheating or the loss of our baby. They also didn't need to know that I wasn't over it.

I called Mr. Olsen and got my summer job back at the marina. I needed something to occupy my time and my mind, so

I worked as many hours as he was willing to give me. I drove by Tyler's house several times, but I never saw his car. I was guessing that he didn't come home for the summer. Except for the few times I saw Tori, I didn't do much but go to work and come home.

I filled my time by hanging out with my parents. My mom was enjoying taking care of me and trying to get me out of my funk. My dad was happy to have me home so we could watch movies together. The rest of the time I spent reading smutty romance novels. That only made me miss Tyler more. This was going to be the worst summer ever.

It was Fourth of July weekend. The marina was crazy. Everyone wanted to take their boats out on the lake. I worked the entire weekend and made a shitload of tips. I even went to a bonfire with some of the other people from the marina. I knew it would make my parents happy that I was getting out and doing something other than moping around the house. I had a good time. I did a little drinking, a little dancing, and some shameless flirting.

My parents had been staying home a lot. Even though I told them I was fine, I think they knew I really wasn't. They went to a Fourth of July party, and I was glad they were finally getting out too. I got home late and was surprised that my parents weren't home yet. They weren't really party people, so one in the morning was late for them.

I heard thunder in the distance and knew one of our wicked summer storms was rolling in. I decided to wait for my parents downstairs instead of going up to my room. I found a *Lifetime* movie on cable and snuggled up on the couch under my favorite cozy blanket. The storm started to kick up. Wind whipped branches against the house and rain lashed at the windows. I snuggled deeper into the couch.

A loud knock at the front door startled me awake. I must have fallen asleep on the couch. I looked at the clock on the cable box, it was after three in the morning. I didn't even hear my parents come in. They must have decided I looked comfortable and let me sleep.

The knock came at the door again, this time louder and more insistent. I jumped off the couch. I didn't want it to wake my parents since they got home so late. I looked out the side window next to the door and saw two uniformed police officers standing on the porch. What the hell did they want?

I cautiously opened the door a crack. "May I help you?"

The taller officer spoke first. "Are you Kyla O'Malley?"

"Yes," I answered. This was kind of freaking me out. I watched a lot of true crime shows where fake police broke into homes and killed people. I didn't want to be one of those helpless victims on television. "What do you want?"

The shorter one spoke this time. "Can we come in?"

Oh, hell no! "Let me go get my parents. I'll be right back." I started to close the door on them.

The tall one put his hand on the door to stop me from closing it. I was definitely freaking out now. "Miss O'Malley, are your parents James and Maria O'Malley?" I nodded. "When was the last time you saw your parents?"

Okay, this was getting weird. "They went out to a party tonight. They're upstairs sleeping."

"Did you see them come home, Miss O'Malley?" The two officers were looking at each other strangely.

"Well, no. I fell asleep on the couch. What's going on?" I asked.

The shorter officer spoke first, "I'm sorry to have to be the one to tell you this. There's been an accident. Your parents were hit by a drunk driver tonight."

My hands went up to cover my mouth as I gasped. "Oh my God! Where are they? Take me to them!" I picked up my purse from the table in the hall. I knew they were out too late. It wasn't like them.

The taller officer put his hand on my shoulder. "I'm sorry. They didn't make it. They were killed on impact."

My legs gave out and I sank to the floor in the hallway. This couldn't be happening. The officers opened the door and helped me to the couch. This wasn't real. It had to be another one of my nightmares. I didn't take my Xanax last night. This was a nightmare. I was sure of it. I just had to wake up. *Wake up, dammit!*

"Miss O'Malley, are you okay? Is there someone we can call for you?" I just stared at these strangers in my house. I had barely heard them talking to me.

I blinked my eyes. "I'm sorry. What did you say?"

"I asked if there was someone we could call for you. We can't leave you alone like this."

I got up and grabbed my phone off the coffee table. "Tori. I can call Tori."

I dialed her number and waited while it rang and rang. Finally, she answered. "Kyla, why in the hell are you calling me in the middle of the night?" I didn't know what to say. "Kyla?"

My voice was emotionless. "Something's happened, Tori. Something bad. Can you come over?"

Tori sounded more awake now. "Kyla, what's going on? Are you okay?"

"Please, just hurry." I hung up. I stared at my parents' wedding picture that sat on the mantle above the fireplace. I looked back at the officers. "Are you sure there hasn't been some mistake? I know they're upstairs sleeping." I rushed up the stairs taking them two at a time. I burst into my parents' room and turned on the light. The bed was neatly made. My mother's nightgown was laid out on her pillow. I turned and walked out of the room and stumbled down the steps. I looked at the officers.

"They're not there." I sat back on the couch and stared at nothing. This couldn't be real.

The front door opened. I heard Tori's voice, "Kyla, why is there a police car…" She looked at the officers and then at me.

I turned and stared at her and Chris. "They're gone."

Tori came and kneeled in front of me. "Who's gone, sweetie?"

I couldn't look her in the eyes. "My parents. They were killed by a drunk driver."

"Oh my God!" She wrapped her arms around me. I didn't hug her back. My arms just hung limply at my sides.

"Jesus Christ," Chris mumbled.

I looked at Tori. "What am I going to do? I'm all alone."

Tori grabbed me by the shoulders. "Kyla, you're not alone. We're your family. We're going to help you." Tori looked at Chris and then back at me. "Do you want us to call Tyler?"

My eyes went wide. "No! This isn't his problem. I'm not his problem anymore."

"Okay, sweetie." Her arms went back around me. I couldn't even cry. I couldn't believe this was happening.

One of the officers turned to Chris. "Sir, can I talk to you in the other room." Chris followed him into the kitchen.

Chris and Tori stayed with me well into the next day. The officer had left Chris with instructions for what I needed to do and who I needed to contact. There were phone calls to make and arrangements to be made. Everything was so surreal.

When they left, I took a Xanax and went to sleep, but nothing could keep the nightmares away.

Chapter 24
Tyler

I had just gotten back from a long ride on my bike. God, she was a beauty. The way she rumbled when I started her up provided a sense of calm I rarely felt anymore. I loved the feel of the open road and the freedom I felt while riding her. If I was being honest, I bought the Harley as a distraction, but every time I rode her all I could think about was the blond that should have been on the back of her.

The distraction wasn't working.

I went inside and set my aviators and helmet on the kitchen table. I grabbed a beer from the fridge and headed out back to sit on the small patio. Sitting back in one chair and putting my feet up on another, I cracked my beer open and took a long swig. I pulled my phone out and checked my missed calls. Several were from Chris. I hadn't talked to him in a couple of weeks.

I pressed his contact and waited. When he picked up, I started razzing him, "Hey, man. I haven't talked to you in a while. Tori got you chained to the bed or something?"

Chris's voice held no humor. "No, man. Sorry I haven't called. I um… I need to tell you something about Kyla."

I sat up straighter in my chair and put my beer on the table. "What's wrong with Kyla? Is she okay?" I wanted to not care, but who was I fooling? I couldn't not care.

Chris let out a big sigh. "She's okay. I mean she's not hurt or anything. It's her parents."

I let out a breath of relief and relaxed back into the chair. "What about her parents?"

"They were killed in a car accident two nights ago."

I sat back up. "Excuse me? What did you just say?"

"Tori got a call from Kyla at three-thirty in the morning. We went over to her house and the police were there. She was just sitting there in shock. It was the saddest goddamn thing I've seen in my life, man. We've spent the last day and a half helping her make phone calls and arrangements. She had to go to the morgue to identify the bodies. She hasn't even cried. She's just accepted the fact that she's alone now. I mean, Tori and I are going to be there for her, but she's right really. She is alone. I'm a little worried about her."

I sat there taking in everything Chris was telling me. "Why didn't she call me?"

"Do you really have to ask? She said she's not your problem anymore. She didn't want to put this on you. I mean you two haven't talked in over four months. She doesn't even know I'm calling you, but I thought you should know."

"Thanks, Chris. Let me know what the arrangements are. I'm coming down for the funeral." I hung up. I couldn't believe I even just said those words. The funeral.

She didn't want to call me. I guess I had done a good job convincing her I didn't care. I wanted her to need me. I wanted her to call me. God, I was fucked up. I had spent the last several months convincing everyone, including myself that I didn't care.

It was all a lie.

Chapter 25
Kyla

All our family lived out of state. The phone calls I had to make were heartbreaking. My father's parents moved to Texas a long time ago, but both had died in the past few years. My mother's parents lived in Missouri. It was an awful phone call. Gram and Gramps were flying in today and were going to be staying with me. My mom's sister and her family were flying in too.

I knew my parents had bought cemetery plots a few years ago, so that was taken care of. I contacted the minister at their church. I went to the funeral home and picked out caskets. Tori and Chris went with me to make all the arrangements. They had been great. I couldn't ask for two better friends. I was lucky to have them.

I sent them home to get some sleep, but I still had to go the florist. And pick out clothes for them to be buried in.

I was sitting at the kitchen table just thinking of all the things I had to do when the house phone rang. I wasn't in the mood to talk on the phone anymore, but I didn't have a choice. It was my dad's attorney. He needed to come talk to me, so I told him to head over.

Arnie was a kind older man. He wasn't just my dad's attorney; he was his friend. Arnie came in and sat at the table with me. "Kyla, I'm sorry to be seeing you again under these circumstances, but I thought you might need a little help."

I looked at him and nodded my head. "I don't know what to do. The house, the cars, I don't even know how I'm going to pay for all of this."

"That's why I'm here. I'm going to help you. Your parents weren't just clients, they were friends. Paying is not going to be a problem. Your parents put you on all their bank accounts and investments when you turned eighteen. There is plenty of money. They left me all the information, so that if anything ever happened, I could give it to you. I just never imagined it would be now, but they were prepared. They didn't want you to struggle."

"They were that prepared? They never talked about it."

"When your dad's parents died a few years ago, your dad had to go through hell to get things straightened out. He dealt with a lot of red tape. He didn't want that for you. I can go with you to the bank to get checks ordered in your name. I have all the proper paperwork, so it won't be a problem."

I got up and gave Arnie a hug, "Thanks, Arnie. This actually helps a lot." I sat back down and started thinking. "What about the house? I go to Western, and I have one year left. I can't be here to take care of it."

"We can handle all of that in a couple of weeks. You can keep it, sell it, or rent it out. It's up to you. You don't have to make any decisions right now. As a matter of fact, I don't think you should decide anything right now. Give it some time."

"How much money is there? I mean, my school is paid for, I have a scholarship, but I'll need to pay for my car insurance, house payments, utilities, and everything for the burial. I'm a little worried. This is so overwhelming."

"Don't worry. Your parents planned well. They did a quit claim deed for the house, so your name will be on it. I can go with you to file the paperwork. As for the money, they have a couple hundred thousand in the bank and about seven hundred thousand in investments."

I leaned back in the chair. "That's more than I expected. How were they able to save that much money? Dad was always so frugal, I just assumed that we had enough, but not that much."

Arnie laughed. "Yeah, your dad was a little cheap, but he was a financial advisor and made good money. He was concerned about retirement though. He saved like crazy so that he and your mom would be able to enjoy retirement without worrying about money."

"I feel weird about this. That money was their nest egg."

"You shouldn't feel guilty, Kyla. They wanted it this way."

Arnie went with me to the bank, and I was thankful that he was helping me. He knew exactly what to do and I was clueless. I promised him that I would call when I had made decisions about the house and cars. Arnie was a God send.

Gram and Gramps arrived later that day, along with my Aunt Kay and her husband, Uncle John. Gram and Gramps helped me finalize all the plans for the funeral, including flowers and clothes for the burial. I felt like a zombie going through the motions. I just kept going through my list of things that needed to be done and checked them off as each was completed.

The day of the funeral arrived. I wore a simple black dress and twisted my hair up in a French knot. I went to my box and took out Tyler's ring. I needed his strength today. I slipped it on my finger and looked down at the shiny, purple heart that stared back at me.

Grams and Gramps sat in the front row of the church with me. They sat on one side of me, Tori and Chris sat on the other side of me. The minister did the service and I heard people around me crying. I still hadn't cried a single tear. It still wasn't real.

I saw Tyler's parents sitting in the back of the church, but not Tyler. He wasn't coming. I hadn't expected him to, but I thought maybe he would show.

Toward the end of the service, the minister motioned to me. I stood and made my way to the front of the church. I had written a farewell to my parents that I would read.

I cleared my voice. "My parents had a special kind of love. They had been together since high school, and I came shortly after. They weren't just husband and wife. They were soul mates, partners, and best friends. They completed each other. When things got tough, they always approached life as a team. I can honestly say, I don't remember a single time they ever said a bad word about each other. They were my example of what love is. I hope that one day, I am lucky enough to find the kind of love they shared. In a way, it was a blessing they died together, because I don't know how one of them would have survived without the other." I looked out at the church full of people and saw Tyler standing in the back. He put his hand to his lips and blew a kiss in my direction. My next words were specifically for him. I didn't look down at what I had written. I didn't need to. "When you find a love that is special, you never give up. You cherish it, you nurture it, you hold it close to your heart. You never know when life has other plans for you, and *down the road* may never come. So, treat each other kindly, love each other as if tomorrow doesn't exist, and never take love for granted. Because a broken heart, is never really whole again."

    I walked back down to the front pew and held the hands of both my Grams and Tori. I had said what was in my heart. I hoped Tyler heard me. The song I had chosen for the funeral started to play, and Carrie Underwood's voice filled the church as she sang "See You Again". The only one not crying was me. I still couldn't.

Chapter 26
Tyler

Kyla's words gutted me. I knew she was talking about her parents, but I felt like she was talking to me. About our love for each other. There was no doubt in my mind that I still loved her.

And that song... I needed to talk to her. But I didn't know if I wanted to go there with her. I was just getting my life back together again.

I followed the procession to the cemetery. I stood in the back and watched as Kyla's parents were lowered into the ground. She stood stoically at the edge of the burial site. I admired her bravery. She was stronger than I remembered a few months ago.

As the gravesite service ended, people began to leave. I stood there and watched her place two red roses on top of the caskets and kiss them goodbye. It was not something I was prepared for. The sadness I felt for her welled up in my chest.

She saw me standing there watching her. She whispered something to her grandparents, and they left. Tori and Chris were standing by her side, and I wished it were me. She talked to them briefly and shot me a glance. Then they walked back to their car, leaving Kyla and me alone.

Kyla walked up to me. "Thank you for coming. I wasn't sure you would." Her eyes were not rimmed with red. I saw no tears ready to fall. She looked absolutely beautiful, except those green eyes. They were blank with dark circles underneath, void of any emotion at all.

I didn't know what to say, so I told her the truth. "I couldn't not come. Your parents were a big part of my life too. I needed to be here." I put my hands in my suit pockets and cocked my head at her. "What are you going to do now?"

"I'm not sure, but I'll figure it out." Kyla looked down at her hands. I noticed that my ring was still on her finger. "Everything has a way of working itself out. How long are you here for?"

"I just came in for the funeral. I'm leaving tomorrow."

She nodded her head. "Well, I'm glad you could come. It would have meant a lot to my parents. They really loved you." She turned to walk away.

I grabbed her arm. "Kyla…" I looked at her with pleading eyes.

She put her hand on mine and gently removed it from her arm. "Tyler, it's okay. I'm going to be fine. This isn't your problem. Go… live your life." Then she walked away from me. From my life. From everything we once had. Like I had done to her.

Chapter 27
Kyla

I was dead inside. I wasn't prepared for dealing with Tyler. I wanted to wrap my arms around his neck and tell him to stay. Instead, I did the selfless thing, and let him go. Just like he did to me all those months ago.

My grandparents and Aunt Kay left the next morning. Gram and Gramps were hesitant to leave me alone, but I really needed them to go. I couldn't stand being hovered over. I promised I would call if I needed anything. I explained to them that Arnie was going to help me take care of everything and that Tori was only a phone call away.

After everyone left, the silence was deafening. I had been so busy the last few days making arrangements, spending time at the funeral home, and then the funeral, that I really hadn't let the reality of my parents' death sink in. The kitchen was full of flowers from the funeral. So many lilies. Why did people send lilies for a funeral? I would never be able to look at one again without thinking about death.

I walked through the quiet rooms of my house and looked at the family pictures on the walls. I ran my hand over them, remembering all the happy times. My mom still had the picture of Tyler and me from prom hanging on the wall. I took it down and stared at us. We looked so young. So much had happened to us since this picture was taken. We were just kids then and now I was being thrown into the world of adulthood without a safety net.

I set the picture down on the coffee table and went up the stairs. I sat on my parents' bed and picked up my mother's nightgown. I ran my fingers over the silky fabric and held it up to my face. I never realized that my mom had a specific smell before, but I could smell her on this nightgown. The first tear fell down my cheek.

I stood and walked to their closet and opened the doors. I looked at all the clothes they would never wear again. I began taking the clothes out and throwing them on the floor as anger took over my body. I grabbed handful after handful and threw them down, ripping things off the hangers as I screamed, "How dare you leave me? I hate you! I hate you! I hate you!" Tears streamed down my face, and I sobbed uncontrollably. The remaining pieces of my heart shattered with every word that left my mouth. I clenched my fists and let out a frustrated scream. I reached back into the closet and pulled out my mother's shoes and started throwing them across the room. They bounced off the walls and crashed to the floor. "Why did you leave me? I hate you! I hate you!"

Suddenly arms wrapped around me from behind. "Kyla! Stop!" I fell to my knees in the middle of the pile of clothes. I cried and cried; the tears kept coming. I let everything I'd been holding in, pour out. Tori held me from behind and rocked me, quietly telling me it would be alright. "I knew this was coming," she said.

I laid down in the clothes. "Everyone keeps leaving me. Tyler, my baby, my parents…why does everyone keep leaving me?"

"I don't know, sweetie. Come on, let's get you out of here." Tori pulled me to my feet.

I looked around at the mess I made. "I need to clean this up." I started picking up the clothes from the floor.

Tori took the clothes from my hand and dropped them back to the floor. "Not today, you don't." She led me from the room and shut the door behind us.

"What are you doing here anyway?" I sniffed as I wiped the tears from my face. I never heard her come in.

"I came to check on you. It was only a matter of time before you finally broke down."

Tori took me down the stairs and to the couch. I sat down and picked up the picture from the coffee table. "We look so young in this picture. What happened to us?" I asked, without expecting her to answer. I put the picture down and pushed it to the side. "I guess it doesn't really matter."

I laid down on the couch and put my head in Tori's lap. "This is gonna suck, isn't it?"

Tori played with the ends of my hair. "Yeah. It is. But you'll get through it, just like everything else."

"I'm tired of getting through it. I don't know how much more I can take." I put my hand over my eyes and dragged it down my face.

Tori looked down at me. "How have you been sleeping?"

"Sleep? What's that?" I joked.

She nodded her head. "That's what I thought. Where are your pills?"

"They're in my bedroom. On the nightstand," I answered.

Tori slipped out from under me and walked up the stairs. When she came back down, she handed me a pill and a glass of water. "You need to get some sleep. Take this. Hopefully, you'll sleep through to the morning."

I took the Xanax and grabbed a blanket from the back of the couch. "I love you, girlfriend. See you tomorrow?"

"Love you, too. I'll come by tomorrow night."

Tori left and I quickly fell asleep.

I woke to the sun beating through the front windows. I rolled over and covered my head with the blanket. I didn't want to get up. Maybe if I ignored everything, it would all just go away. I didn't have to go back to work for another week, so I could just lay here all day if I wanted to.

After about ten minutes of arguing with myself, I finally got up off the couch. I stretched and walked over to the window to look out. Damn! I hadn't realized how long the grass had gotten. I guess that would be my challenge for the day. I had never cut the grass before. I didn't even know how to start the mower.

I went to the fridge to get a glass of orange juice. I pulled out the jug and there were just a few swigs left, so I drank right from the bottle. The fridge was practically empty. I guess grocery shopping was on the list for today too.

I went upstairs to change and then headed out back to the shed. I pulled the mower out and stared at it. I was a smart girl. I could figure this out. I pulled the cord, and nothing happened. I tried again, this time holding down the bar on the handle. Again, nothing. Well, this is just stupid! How hard could it be to start a damn lawnmower?

I pulled out my phone and called Chris. "Hey, Kyla, what's up?"

"I know this is going to sound really stupid, but… how do you start a lawnmower?"

Chris let out a laugh. "You've never cut the grass before? Do you want me to come do it for you?"

"No, I can do it. I just need to know how to start this damn thing. I pulled the cord, and nothing happened." I kicked the grass in frustration.

"Did you prime it first?"

"What does that mean?" I asked.

"There should be a little rubber button somewhere by the cord. You need to push it three or four times to get the gas into the motor. Then hold the handle and pull the cord."

I saw the button he was talking about. "Okay, I see it. Thanks, Chris. I'll call you back if I still can't get this stupid machine started." I hung up, pushed the button four times, held the handle, and pulled the cord. The lawnmower roared to life. I did a little fist pump and started mowing.

After I finished mowing the grass, I went in and took a shower. I was disgusting. I decided that mowing the grass was not one of my favorite jobs. After my shower, I headed to the grocery store. I really didn't know what to buy and I couldn't see myself doing a lot of cooking for only one person. I got the basics. Milk, bread, cereal, fruit… anything that was easy.

As I headed home from the grocery store, I passed a liquor store. I made an impulsive decision, turned the car around and headed back. I walked into the store and looked at all the bottles behind the counter. I really didn't know what I wanted. The guy behind the counter seemed impatient. "What can I get you?"

"Umm…give me a fifth of Captain Morgan's and a fifth of that strawberry vodka." I pointed at the shelf behind him.

"Having a party?" the guy asked.

"Yeah…party for one. Hold on a sec." I went down the aisle and grabbed a 2-liter of diet Coke and a bottle of Sprite. I placed them on the counter.

"Anything else?" he asked.

What the fuck? Why not? "Give me a pack of Marlboro Light 100s." I didn't know much about cigarettes, but I'd seen other girls smoking these, so they must be okay. I grabbed a purple lighter and placed it on the counter too. "That's it," I said.

When I got home, I stuck a pizza in the oven, made myself a drink and sat on the couch. I flipped through the channels and stopped on *Sports Center* when I saw Tyler's picture. They were talking about the upcoming college football season. Ty was getting all kinds of praise from the sportscasters, and he was predicted to be in the running for the Heisman Trophy. I let out a little smile. Even if we weren't together, I was still proud of all that he'd accomplished.

The oven timer went off and I took my pizza out on the back patio to eat. I called Tori to check in. She wanted to come over, but I told her I needed a night to myself. I didn't tell her I planned on getting shit-faced drunk. I deserved it. It was a gift to myself.

After dinner, I took my purchases from the liquor store and put them on the patio table. The sun was going down, but the air was still warm from the hot July day we'd had. I grabbed a radio and my kindle and sat down at the table. I poured myself a vodka and Sprite, then opened the pack of cigarettes. I took a drink and lit my first cigarette. Let the party begin!

Chapter 28
Tyler

I planned on going home yesterday, but I couldn't make myself leave without talking to Kyla first. Seeing her the other day, damn near broke me. I knew we couldn't be together, but the way we had left things didn't sit well with me. There was so much left unsaid. Who the fuck was I kidding? I missed the hell out of her. I needed to know she would be okay.

I drove to her house and went up to the front door. The lights were on, and her car was in the driveway, so I was pretty sure she was home. I knocked and waited. No one answered, so I knocked again. I could hear music on, so I walked around the back of the house.

I saw Kyla, sitting there in the dark, staring out into the yard. She had a drink in one hand and cigarette in the other. I watched as she took a drag off the cigarette and blew the smoke up into the air. I walked over and sat in the chair next to her. "Hey."

She looked at me, took a sip of her drink, and looked back out into the yard. "I thought you were going home yesterday?" She downed the rest of her drink.

"I was, but I decided to stay an extra couple of days." I looked at the liquor bottles on the table. She had put quite a dent in the vodka bottle.

Kyla stubbed out her cigarette and got up to make herself another drink. "Why is that?" Her demeanor was cold. Her eyes were glassy, and I knew she'd had a good buzz going.

I leaned forward with my arms on my knees. "I don't know. I needed to see you, I guess. Make sure you were okay."

She sat back down with her new drink and lit another cigarette. She took a long drag and blew out the smoke. "As you can see, I'm doing just fine."

I reached over, took the cigarette out of her hand, and stubbed it out on the ground. "Are you? You're out here drinking by yourself and smoking. That's not you."

"People change, Tyler. I'm sorry if you don't approve, but I don't really need your approval anymore." She looked at me questioningly. "Why are you really here?"

I ran my hand through my hair. "Dammit, Ky, I miss you! There! I said it!"

Her eyes softened, and her demeanor changed instantly. "I miss you too. I've missed you every fucking day for the last four and a half months."

I looked at the bottles on the table. "I think I need a drink. May I?"

She waved her hand at the table. My ring was gone from her finger. "Help yourself. You know where the glasses are. I think there's some beer in the fridge too if you'd rather."

I got up from the table and walked into the kitchen. I opened the fridge and pulled out a beer. I cracked the top and took a long drink. I looked around the kitchen that was full of flowers from the funeral. I'd spent a lot of time here. Her dad had the sex talk with us at that kitchen table. I smiled remembering how mortified Kyla had been. I picked up a pill bottle from the kitchen counter and read the label. Xanax? This had been prescribed to her before her parents died. What the fuck have I done to her?

I set the pills back down and grabbed another beer from the fridge. I was going to need it. Kyla sipped her drink and had lit another cigarette. The radio was playing "Trying Not to Love You". She was lost in thought, staring off into space.

I sat back down. "You okay?"

"Yeah, just thinking... We danced to this song at Homecoming."

"I remember." I remembered that night perfectly. That was the night I got the courage up to kiss her and make her my girlfriend. She'd been so flustered that she blurted out that she was a virgin. It was seven months later that we lost our virginity to each other. God, those months had been torture. I wanted her so bad. "So... what'd you do today?"

"Oh, banner day around here. I cut the grass for the first time." She waved her hand around to the yard. "Grocery shopping, just normal, everyday stuff."

I laughed. "You cut the grass? Do you even know how to start the mower?"

She gave me the evil eye. "I called Chris. He talked me through it. I can do shit, you know." She took a deep breath and blew it out. "I have a feeling I'm going to be learning how to do a whole bunch of things I've never done before."

"Yeah, probably." I stared off, thinking about all the responsibilities she would have. "What are you going to do with the house?"

"I don't know yet. Maybe rent it out. I'm not ready to sell it. There are too many memories here. This is the only home I've ever known. My dad's friend slash attorney is going to help me out with everything. Arnie's a good guy. He won't steer me wrong. I'm going to sell their cars though. I can't drive three cars."

It was so much to think about. I was surprised she could talk about everything so matter-of-factly. "Renting it out is probably a good idea. It'll give you time to decide what you really want to do."

"Yeah, I think so. You know what's so weird? They already had my name on everything. The house, bank accounts, investments... it's like they knew."

"Kyla?"

"Hmmm?"

"Why didn't you call me when this happened?" I needed to hear it from her.

"By 'this', you mean my parents dying? It's okay. You can say it." She turned her chair to face me. "Do you really want to know? You might not like what I have to say."

I reached forward and pulled her chair closer to mine, so we were knee-to-knee. "Yeah, I really want to know."

She pulled her legs up on the chair and sat cross-legged. "Because I've spent every day for the last four and half months trying not to think about you. Because I miss my best friend. Because you left me at the hospital without saying goodbye. Because when I see you, I think about our baby. Because I know you've moved on. Because I know you've been with other girls since you left. Because I can't use you as a crutch to deal with my problems anymore. And most importantly, because I still love you and you don't love me, and I couldn't face rejection. I've lost too much already." She dropped her head.

I raised my eyebrows. That was more than I expected. "Wow, that's a lot of reasons, but you're wrong about one thing." I leaned forward and held her face. "I still love you."

She turned her head in my hands. "Don't say it if you don't mean it. I can't take it."

I put my finger under her chin and turned her face back to mine. I looked deep into her green eyes that I missed so much. "I mean it." I leaned in and kissed her soft lips. God, I missed that. "I'm not over you. I've tried. I've tried every distraction I could think of. And nothing seems to work. You're so far under my skin that you're a part of me."

"I'm sorry I hurt you. I was wrong not to tell you about our baby. I said a lot of nasty things to you. I was mad and should have never said the things I said to you." She gave me a soft, gentle kiss.

"I'm sorry I made it so impossible to tell me. You were right, I wasn't ready to hear it at the time, but if you hadn't miscarried, I would have been there. We could have made it work. I think about our baby too. About what could have been." I kissed her a little deeper this time.

She pulled back and smiled. "I would have been waddling around like a penguin right now."

I smiled back at her. "You would have been cute as hell." I reached my arms under her ass and pulled her onto my lap. "I'm sorry I left without saying goodbye. It was the hardest thing I've ever done."

She ran her hands through my hair. "I understand why you did it. I would have never let you go." She pressed her lips to mine, and I pushed my tongue inside. I kissed her deeply and wrapped my arms around her, pulling her closer. She broke the kiss. I rested my head on her chest, as her arms came around the back of my neck.

She ran her hands through my hair again and then pulled back. She whispered to me, "I know this doesn't mean we're back together, but can we just pretend for tonight?"

"Yeah, I'd love that." I kissed her again and poured my whole heart into it. Our tongues tangled together as I rubbed her ass. She rubbed her heat into my hardness. "Kyla, I want you."

"Take me to bed, Ty." I lifted her off the chair and she wrapped her legs around me. I carried her into the house and shut the door behind us. She smiled down at me as I carried her up the stairs to her bedroom.

I laid her down on the bed and reached over my shoulder to pull my shirt off. This was the first time Kyla would see my tattoos. She sat up and rubbed her hand over my heart. The words *We Loved with a Love That was More Than Love* were scripted on my chest. "Edgar Allen Poe," she whispered. "I remember it from World Lit senior year." She ran her hand along the outside of my left arm. A football and helmet were tattooed there with the words *For the Love of the Game*. I turned so she could see my back. A giant Celtic cross took up most of it. "They're sexy, Tyler. You been working out?" She smirked.

"I need something to take up my time. You like?"

"I love it." She ran her hand over my chest again, focusing on the words there. "Make love to me."

I kneeled between her legs and reached for the hem of her shirt. I slowly pulled it up over her head. She was my dream, my addiction, and my worst weakness all in one package. I reached behind her back, unclasped her bra, and slid it down her arms. Her tits were perfect. Her nipples were hard, begging me to suck on them. "I've missed these." I reached up and massaged her tits. They filled my hands and felt like heaven.

"Suck my tits, Tyler." She arched her back and pushed them toward my face. I leaned forward and took one in my mouth, twirling my tongue around the hard peak. Kyla let out a gasp and I moved to the other one.

She unbuttoned her shorts and pushed them down her legs. Laying there in only her black thong, she was gorgeous. I ran my hands from her waist and down her slender legs. She looked skinnier. I frowned at her. "You've lost weight."

"A little," she admitted.

"Don't lose anymore or all these gorgeous curves are going to disappear. And that would be a crime."

She giggled. "I'll keep that in mind."

I unbuttoned my shorts and slid them off. I reached into the pocket and pulled out my wallet. I took out a condom and held it up.

"I'm on the pill, it's up to you."

I threw the condom over my shoulder. I might have regretted it later, but I needed to feel my girl. Having a baby with Kyla, didn't scare me anymore.

I laid between her legs, holding myself up with my arms. I kissed her lips, and she tangled her hands in my hair. I kissed down her neck, the valley between her breasts, and down her stomach. She arched up into my kisses. I loved how responsive she always was to my touch. I hooked my fingers in her thong and slid it off.

She opened her legs for me, inviting me in. I slid my tongue down between her folds to her pussy. I stuck my tongue into her opening and tasted her. She tasted so sweet. It was the best thing I'd had in my mouth in months. I hadn't done this to anyone but Kyla... ever. I ate her out with desperation. Kyla's hips bucked off the bed. I placed my hand on her stomach and pushed her back to the mattress. I licked up to her clit, stroking her sensitive spot with the tip of my tongue. She gripped the comforter in her fists and threw her head back, "Oh my God, it's been too long. Make me come, Ty!"

It was all I needed to hear. I sucked her clit into my mouth. Kyla's hands pressed on the back of my head, pushing me into her. I sucked and nuzzled her clit. When I knew she was close, I pulled back and stuck two fingers into her wet pussy. I pumped them in and out, slowing twisting and bending my fingers inside her, until she was begging for more. With my fingers still deep inside her, I brought my mouth back to her clit and sucked. I sucked and sucked until I felted her pussy start to tighten around my fingers. Kyla's breathing became fast and shallow as she was about to fall over the edge. "It's too much!" I went in for the kill, pumped her hard and gave her clit one more long suck with my mouth, using my tongue to touch her just where she needed it. Kyla threw her head back and screamed my name as she shattered. Her body writhed on the bed and her pussy clenched my fingers in wave after wave of pleasure.

As she began to come down, I crawled up her body. I gave her a gentle kiss and looked into those green eyes. "You're so beautiful when you come."

She wrapped her arms around my shoulders. "Oh my God, I forgot how amazing that is. How you make me feel. It's been so long."

"I don't want you to ever forget how good we are together. This is something we always got right."

She gave me a genuine smile. "Yeah, we did. Didn't we?" She pushed on my shoulder, and I fell to my back beside her laughing.

She climbed on top of me, straddling my waist. I took her face in my hands. "I love you, Kyla. I've never stopped."

"Believe me, I've never stopped loving you either." She leaned forward and sensually kissed the tattoo on my chest.

"This one is my favorite." She slid back down my body, 'til she was straddling my legs. She tugged on the top of my boxer briefs, and I lifted my hips to help her slide them off. She threw them on the floor next to the rest of our clothes.

Kyla looked at me from under her eyelashes as she licked the drop of precum from the tip of my dick. God, I'd missed her mouth. She ran her tongue around the rim of the head, teasing me. She rubbed her hand gently up and down my shaft, pumping me from base to tip. Finally, thank God, Kyla opened her mouth and took me in. Her lips suctioned tight around my dick as she bobbed up and down, her tongue swirling over every inch of me. I growled when she opened her throat and took me deeper, swallowing so her throat clenched my dick again and again. "Baby, you gotta stop." She slid her mouth up and released me with a pop, a wicked smile on her face.

Kyla sat up and ran her nails up and down my chest. "Last chance to change your mind about the condom."

I shook my head. "Not a chance, baby. I want to feel you."

Kyla hovered above me and I lined myself up with her pussy. She sank down on my dick and I groaned. Her eyes closed, and her hands went to my chest. She arched her back and moved her hips forward, sliding up and then sank back down me. "Ky, that feels incredible. I love being able to feel you skin on skin. Your so wet." She arched her back again, pushing her tits forward along with her hips. I reached up and took them in my hands, rubbing my thumbs over her nipples. She threw her head back as she continued to ride me. I wasn't going to last long at this rate.

I wrapped my arms around her tiny waist and flipped her onto her back. I braced myself on one arm and pressed my lips to hers. She opened for me, and our tongues twisted together. While we continued to kiss, I pushed deep inside her. She was so tight and so wet. I took my time and made love to her slowly. Her hips moved with mine, meeting me thrust for thrust. Kyla wrapped her legs around me and I picked up the pace. I was so close. "Do you want me to pull out?" I didn't want to, but I had to ask.

"No way," she gasped. "Harder, Ty. Harder."

I slammed into her over and over again. I felt her pussy tighten around my dick as she found her release. Her pussy clenched me with each wave of her orgasm. I thrusted two more times and fell over the edge with her. It was the first time I had ever emptied everything inside her without a condom and it felt amazing. I collapsed my head against her chest, breathing heavily.

I lifted my head to look at Kyla. She opened her eyes and had a very satisfied look on her face. She started to rub her nails up and down my back. She whispered, "That was… there are no words. I've missed you so much."

"I've missed you too. You're so tight, baby. When's the last time you've… you know?" I asked. Now probably wasn't the time, since I was still inside her, but I needed to know.

"Had sex? It's been a while."

I quirked an eyebrow up at her, silently asking her to elaborate.

She rolled her eyes at me. "Six months, okay. It's only ever been you. You're the only one I've ever let touch me."

Well, if that didn't make me feel good and like shit at the same time. I'd had sex so many times since we broke up that I'd lost count. She turned her head to the side to hide the tear that ran down her cheek. I ran my thumb over her face and wiped the tear away. "It's okay, Ky." I pulled out and rolled to the side. I wrapped her in my arms, and she snuggled into my chest.

"You probably think I'm pathetic. I just couldn't do it."

I squeezed her a little tighter. "I don't think your pathetic. I think you're amazing." I kissed the top of her head. We laid there in silence, just enjoying being wrapped up in each other. I finally broke the silence. "I know this might be out of line, but can I stay the night with you?"

"Yeah, I'd love for you to stay." She set her chin on my chest. "I haven't gotten my fill of you yet."

"Oh yeah?" I smiled down at her.

"Not even close." She rolled out of my arms. "Let me go grab a towel." I watched her perfect ass sway to the bathroom. I pulled back the covers and crawled under the sheets. She returned with a towel and threw it at my chest. I wiped myself clean and patted the bed next to me. She slipped in with me.

We laid on our sides facing each other, heads resting on our hands. "They were talking about you on *Sports Center* today," she said.

I chuckled. "You were watching *Sports Center*?"

"I was flipping through the channels, and I saw your picture. I had to watch. They said you're being considered for the Heisman Trophy this year."

"They're just talking, Kyla. It's a long season. Anything can happen."

"Stop being so humble. I'm proud of you. Of everything you've accomplished. You're really going to do this aren't you? Go pro, I mean."

"I hope so... I don't know if I've ever thanked you." Kyla tilted her head to the side, like she didn't understand what I meant, so I continued. "You've been there for me from the beginning. You've always supported me and been my biggest fan." I repeated the words she had used all those years ago. "I couldn't have done it without you."

She rolled her eyes. "Sure, you could have. You have all the talent, I just cheered you on."

"Will you come to my games this year?"

She looked down. "I can't, Tyler. Not if we're not together. It would be too hard for me."

I lifted her chin. "I get that, but it won't be the same without you."

"I'll watch you on TV. It's the best I can do."

"As long as I know you're watching." She got a thoughtful look on her face and her eyebrows narrowed a bit. "What's going on in that pretty little head of yours?"

"Things are really going to be different this year. Different than I thought they would be. I always thought I would be by your side." I ran my finger down the side of her face. "I know that we're not getting back together and I'm glad we cleared the air between us tonight. I just don't know what happened to us. The hardest part of accepting our breakup was the way we ended it, all the anger that was between us. I felt like we never had the closure we needed. I'm not mad anymore and I hope you're not either."

"I'm not mad. I was for a long time, but not anymore. I think all the time we were spending apart because of school, finally took its toll on us. We made it a lot longer than most people in long distance relationships." I took a deep breath and continued. "I let football become more important than you. I know I always said I wouldn't, but I did. I let it take up all my time and there was so little left for us. I took it for granted that you would always be there and then I fucked up."

"I fucked up too. I should have told you the truth. I was scared, and I felt so alone. I wanted to tell you so bad, and then it was too late."

"I don't want you to be scared to tell me anything. I'm sorry I made it so hard for you and you went through all of that by yourself. I know you're on the pill, but if something did happen because of tonight, I need you to know I'm not afraid of having a baby with you anymore. I'd be by your side."

"I know that now. Where do we go from here? There's still something between us, besides great sex obviously." Kyla put her hand on the tattoo over my heart. "I know you feel it too."

"Yeah, I feel it. But... I honestly don't know. I'll always love you. I couldn't stop if I wanted to. I've tried. I think we were meant to be together. Someday. Now just isn't the right time for us."

She leaned forward and placed a gentle kiss on my lips. "At least we have tonight."

"We have tonight."

We made love through the night and into the early morning. We fell asleep wrapped in each other's arms. This night would be burned into my memory forever.

Chapter 29
Kyla

I never expected Tyler to show up last night. I have to admit, I was pissed at first, and thought he was going to toy with my emotions. But I felt like we finally got to say all the things that needed to be said without the anger and yelling. Tyler and I made love all night long. It felt so good being in his arms again, even if I knew it wasn't going to last. The way that boy touched me... I can't even explain.

His new tattoos were sexy as hell and looked good on him. The words printed over his heart, touched me deep inside. We did love each other with a love that was more than love. They made me think of getting my own tattoo. I could pretty much do whatever I wanted now that my parents were gone, and I wouldn't have to face their disapproval.

In the morning, Tyler and I made love one more time. We made our peace with each other, but I wasn't ready for it to end.

"I don't want to let you go, but I know I have to." I gave him a playful shove. "So get out of my bed before I regret this." I laughed.

Tyler pinned me against the mattress with my arms above my head. "I don't regret it. I don't regret a single minute I've ever spent with you."

"Me neither. Now shut up and kiss me." Tyler's lips met mine with so much emotion that it took my breath away. When we finally came up for air, I was breathless. "Wow! Kiss me again." He did. This time it was gentle and tender.

"We should get dressed or I'll never leave this bed," he said.

We got dressed in our clothes from last night and walked down the stairs hand in hand. I stopped on the bottom step so that Tyler and I were closer in height. I wrapped my arms around his shoulders and gave him a soul searing kiss.

"Kyla, you know you can call me, right? If you need anything or just want to talk."

"What if I need you to kill a spider for me?

Tyler gave me that dimpled smile. "Yes."

"What if I just want you to fuck me?"

He laughed. "Even if you just want me to fuck you."

"Promise?"

"Promise."

"I love you, Tyler Jackson."

"I love you, Kyla O'Malley." Tyler squeezed me tight, and our lips locked again.

The front door opened, and Tori's voice rang through the hallway. "Kyla? Is that Tyler's car… Oh, Christ!"

Tyler and I released each other from our embrace, and we held hands as I walked him to the door past a stunned Tori. We gave each other one final kiss and said our goodbyes. Tyler waved at Tori over my shoulder. "Hi, Tori. Bye, Tori." And then he was gone.

"What the hell was that? Are you two back together?"

I had a shit-eating grin on my face. "Nope."

"No? It sure as hell looked like it. What was he doing here?"

I walked past Tori into kitchen to make coffee. "He stopped over last night."

Tori followed me into the kitchen. "Last night? You let him stay the night?"

I reached up in the cabinet and pulled out two coffee cups. "Yes. He stayed the night."

"Did you call him?" she asked.

I turned and leaned back against the counter. "He just showed up. At first, I was pissed that he would just show up here, but it ended up being really good. We talked about all the things we should have talked about months ago."

"But you're not together?" I shook my head. "Did you guys have sex?" I nodded and then turned to fill our cups with coffee. I carried them to the table and got the sugar and creamer. We sat down and Tori eyed me over her cup. "Do you think that was a good idea?"

"It was an awful idea," I admitted. "But what that boy does to my body… Mmmm."

"You're way too happy right now. You know you're going to regret this later, right?"

I shrugged my shoulders. "Maybe, maybe not, probably… hell, I don't know. How could I pass up sex like that? Tori, it's been six months. I was starting to get cobwebs down there."

She giggled, "Damn girl! I can't imagine six months without sex. Was it everything you remembered?"

I smiled smugly. "That, and more." I sipped my coffee. "You know what? I kind of feel a sense of closure now. I can't help but think that we will end up together eventually. But for now, I'm okay."

"You sure?"

"I'm sure. Maybe it's the post-sex bliss talking, but I feel good." I got up to refill my coffee, then sat back down and changed the subject. I didn't want her analyzing my relationship with Ty. Or lack of relationship. "I think I'm going to rent the house out. I mean I'm going to be living in the dorms and I don't want to worry about the utilities and yard maintenance. The grass is going to have to be cut and the snow shoveled. I'm not ready to sell it, so I think this is my best option."

"What about the furniture and stuff?"

I shrugged, "I'll rent it fully furnished. I'll just have to pack up all the personal items. I can probably store them in the basement. I'll talk to Arnie about it."

It was weird living in the house all by myself. I always slept with the TV on because every little sound freaked me out. My sleeping habits still sucked. If I didn't take Xanax, the nightmares plagued me. But since I had seen Tyler, the nightmares changed. I didn't dream about him leaving me anymore. I dreamt of being alone. Of someone breaking in the house. Of being chased. I would wake up gasping in a cold sweat. Xanax became a necessary part of my nighttime routine.

During the day, I went to work at the marina. I really didn't need the money, but I needed the distraction. When I came home from work, I worked on packing up the house. The first room I tackled was my parents'. I cleaned up the mess I made, folding the clothes and putting them in bags for donation. It made me sad, and I cried often, but it needed to be done.

I took the pictures off the walls, wrapped them in tissue paper and gently placed them in a box. I labeled the box and placed it in the hallway. I emptied the curio cabinets and labeled the box. The bathroom was a disaster. I threw most of it away and kept a small box of things I thought I could use.

Tori stopped over while my head was in the cabinet under the bathroom sink. "Wow, you're really making great progress."

I banged my head on the pipes under the sink. "Shit, Tori! You've got to quit sneaking up on me." I pulled my head out from under the sink and rubbed the top of it.

"Sorry. I can't believe how much you've got done."

"Hell. I've got nothing but time and I need to get this done before school starts. Arnie found a renter for me. Some guy that got transferred here. He works for Chrysler, I think. Anyway, he and his wife are moving in the beginning of September, and they have a baby on the way."

"It looks like you're in good shape. Do you need help?" Tori offered.

I wiped my hands off on my shorts. "Well, Purple Heart is coming tomorrow so I need to put all those bags on the porch for donation. Do you think Chris would help me move some of these boxes down to the basement? Oh, and I still have to go though some of the things in the kitchen."

"Sure. I'll call Chris and see if he can come over."

"Thanks," I said. "I could do it, but some of the boxes are kind of heavy."

Tori and I made quick work of the kitchen. Arnie had said the renters didn't have much, so I left the majority of the things, only packing up items with sentimental value and what I would need for school. Chris carried all the boxes to the basement and stacked them neatly in one corner. With their help, I was getting closer and closer to being finished.

When we were done for the night, the three of us sat out on the patio to have drink.

"I really appreciate you guys helping me. This situation has been a little overwhelming. I don't know how I would have done it without you two," I said.

Chris took another sip of his beer. "Honestly, Kyla, we haven't done that much. You've done all the work, but we were glad to help you. You've handled this better than either one of us expected."

"Well, I didn't have much of a choice. We have to move into the dorms in a couple of weeks and I won't be here to deal with stuff," I answered.

Tori got a weird look on her face and then gave Chris a quick glance. "We kind of wanted to talk to you about that," she said.

I looked between the two of them. "What's going on?" Something strange was happening that they didn't want to tell me about.

Chris looked at Tori and raised his eyebrows. Tori was apprehensive. She reached into her pocket and pulled out a ring. She put it on her finger and held up her hand. "Chris and I got engaged."

I jumped up out of my seat. "Oh my, God!" I gave Tori and Chris each a hug. "Congratulations! I'm so happy for you two!"

"Really? I thought you would be bummed," Tori said.

"Bummed? Why would I be bummed out? You two have been together forever. You totally deserve this."

"Well, with everything that happened between you and Tyler, I just wasn't sure how you'd react."

I waved a hand at her. "Pffft! That has nothing to do with you two. I'm happy for you." Okay, I was a little jealous. I thought Ty and I would be engaged by now, but that ship had sailed.

Chris spoke first. "Kyla, we're not going back to the dorms. We rented an apartment off campus."

"Oh." I couldn't keep the disappointment out of my voice. "That's fine. I'm sure my new roommate will be fine." I tried to sound upbeat, but I was afraid I was failing miserably.

Tori was quick to interject. "We got a two bedroom. We want you to move in with us."

My wheels were spinning. All of this was too much on top of everything else. "I don't think that's a good idea," I said. "I mean you two are starting a new life together. You don't need me hanging around. You're going to want your privacy. Thanks, but I'll figure something out."

"Kyla, we want you to move in with us. We'll have plenty of space. It's all good," Chris tried to convince me.

I looked between the two of them. "Are you sure? I don't want to impose."

"We're sure," they said at the same time.

I think they both felt sorry for me, and I didn't want their pity. "I'll think about it. Can I let you know tomorrow?"

Tori grabbed my hands. "Of course. I know what you think. We're worried about you being alone, and yeah, we are, but I really think this is a good idea. I want my sister with me."

"That would be fun but let me think about it. I just... I feel weird about this." I was so taken off guard by this whole situation. I didn't know what to do.

Two days later I made some decisions. I told Tori and Chris I would move in with them, even though I felt like a third wheel. The thought of going back to the dorms by myself and having a new roommate was awful. I needed my friends. I made a promise to myself, that I would try to give them as much privacy as possible.

I sold both of my parents' cars. I was going to use the money from the cars to put toward a new car when I graduated. The money from their cars and mine would be enough to get something I would really like. It would be a graduation gift to myself.

I also decided that I was getting a tattoo. I knew what I wanted. I had given it a lot of thought since I'd seen Tyler. I drew up the design and went to a shop I had heard was reputable. The guy behind the counter was tall, muscular, cute, and covered in tattoos and piercings. I nervously walked up to the counter. "I want to get a tattoo."

"I'm Zack," he offered. Then he looked me up and down. "You a virgin?" My eyes went wide at his question, and I could feel the redness creeping up my neck. What the hell? Zack laughed. "I mean, is this your first tattoo?"

The blush that was creeping up my cheeks started to recede. "Yeah. First one."

"Cool. What did you have in mind?" I showed him my design. "Who drew this for you?"

"I did."

"You got some talent, girl. I could use someone like you around here. You got a portfolio or anything. I'd love to see what else you can do." Zack waved me around the counter. "Come on back and we'll get started."

We got to a back room, and I sat up on the table. "Yeah. I'm majoring in graphic design and advertising, but I'm going back to Western in a week or so."

"That's too bad. When you come back, come see me." Zack started getting things ready and rolled a stool over to where I was sitting. "Where do you want this?"

I rubbed the place on the back of my left shoulder. "I think right here."

Zack nodded his head. "I'll need you to take your shirt off and lay down on the table. I'll just pull your bra strap down. It'll be sore for a couple of days, so just be careful when you get dressed."

I felt weird taking my shirt off in front of Zack, but I did it and quickly laid down, so I didn't feel so exposed. He pulled my strap down and laid the template on my shoulder. When he was finished, he had me get up and look in the mirror to see if I liked the placement. I got my first glimpse of what my tattoo was going to look like. It was beautiful. "I like it," I said with a smile. I laid back down on the table and tensed up, waiting for the pain.

"Relax, girl. It's going to sting a little at first, but you'll get used to it. The more relaxed you are, the easier it will be for you and me."

I took a deep breath. "Okay. I'm ready."

Zack started the tattoo gun up and it buzzed to life. When it first touched my skin, I flinched. "Easy there." Zack's voice was soothing, and he started to talk to me while he worked. It helped to take my mind off the sting. He was right. After a while, I forgot all about the needle going in and out of my shoulder.

Three hours later, Zack was wiping the last of the ink and blood from my shoulder. "This looks kick-ass. You ready to see it?"

I nodded. "Yeah. I can't wait." I went over to the mirror and looked. It was exactly what I wanted and more beautiful than I had imagined. It was two hearts intertwined, with roses wrapped around it. The roses formed another heart that wrapped around the first two hearts. The colors of the hearts and roses were vibrant reds, pinks, and purples. I had made sure that the roses had thorns to represent the pain that love brings. The thorns punctured the intertwined hearts in three places, where drops of blood dripped. Each puncture represented a loss in my life. One for Tyler, one for my baby, and one for my parents. Scripted over the top were the words *True Love Never Dies*. I turned and faced Zack. "I love it! If you have time, I want two more things."

Zack laughed. "You're addicted already? What do you want?"

"I want an infinity symbol, with the word 'Love', on the inside of my wrist and I want my belly button pierced."

"That's cool. I got time. Want to do it right now? It won't take long."

"Yeah. Let's do it!"

An hour later I had a silver ring with a purple stone through my belly button and an infinity symbol on the inside of my right wrist. Zack bandaged my tattoos and gave me the aftercare instructions. I promised Zack I would be back next week. I had another idea for a design. I just had to draw it up.

Chapter 30
Tyler

Seeing Kyla again, holding her in my arms, making love to her... solidified the fact that I wasn't over her. I wanted her back in my life, but dammit the timing sucked. Football practice had started again and that took up most of my time. We couldn't be back together, just to fall into the same cycle again.

I'm not gonna lie. It hurt when Kyla said she wouldn't come to my games. She had been at every home game since senior year of high school. Knowing she wasn't going to be in the stands cheering me on, was like being punched in the chest.

I sat on my bed, thinking about her. Wondering if she was thinking about me. I thought about that ring sitting in the back of my drawer. She was everything I ever wanted in a woman, and I kept her at arm's length. I shook my head at my own stupidity.

Being with Kyla back in July had made one thing very clear to me. The boozing and the women had to stop. When she told me that she hadn't been with anyone else but me... I was happy. I shouldn't have been, but I was. I knew I was being a hypocrite. If she knew how many girls I had fucked, it would break her heart. Thinking about her with other guys, pissed me off. I was naïve to think that she would never be with someone else. In my heart, she would always be mine. I was just too chicken shit to tell her.

Cody had moved in once football practice started. I loved living alone, but it was cool to have someone else here to bullshit and share a beer with. Since it was our senior year, we were busy with practice and the pressure was intense. It didn't leave a lot of time for anything else.

Kyla was right about the Heisman Trophy. Coach called me into his office to discuss it. Not only would it be huge for me, but also for Michigan State. Winning that trophy would secure me as the number one draft pick for the NFL. I was so damn close to my dream; I could almost touch it. When it happened, I knew one thing for sure. I wanted Kyla by my side. I just hoped she would still be around, and I hadn't pushed her too far away.

Toward the end of August, I got a text from her. I had just walked in from football practice when my phone buzzed. I looked at it and laughed.

Ky: Can you kill a spider for me?
Ty: Always! Where are you?
Ky: On my way to Western. Not that far from MSU.
Ty: Wait, is this a metaphorical spider?
Ky: Yes! You up for it?
Ky: It's cool if you're busy or not interested.
Not interested? Was she crazy?
Ty: I'm interested! I need to take a shower. How long until you get here?
Ky: About a half hour.

I texted her the address. I didn't want her to know about my Harley yet, so I moved it to the end of the parking lot. I hadn't told her about my trust fund. I didn't know why, but I wasn't ready for her to know about it yet. After moving my bike, I ran in to take a shower, and let Cody know she was coming over.

"That's cool," Cody said. "You two getting back together?"

"Nah. We're just hanging out."

"Whatever, man. I can tell by the look on your face that you're not over her yet. Why are you fighting it? Or is she the one putting on the breaks?"

I rubbed my hands over my face. "Honestly? I don't know what we are or where this is going. All I know is that I can't pass up this opportunity to see her. This is the first time she's reached out to me since our breakup. She's going through a lot of shit right now and I don't want to put any pressure on her."

"Be careful, man," Cody warned. "Just don't hurt her. She's the best thing that ever happened to you. If you lead her on again…"

"I'm not," I insisted. "She knows what this is. We both do."

"If you say so." Cody grabbed a beer, went in his room, and shut the door.

Thirty-five minutes later Kyla was at my door. She walked in and looked around. "This is really nice. Do you live here by yourself, or do you have a roommate?"

"Cody moved in once football season started. It's nice not living in the dorms. We have so much more room."

Kyla fidgeted, shuffling from one foot to the other. "I'm sorry I sprung this on you. I was on my way back to school and I was so close…"

I put my finger over her lips. "Shhh. You don't have to apologize or give me a reason. I'm glad you called."

She let out a big breath and I saw her visibly relax. "Yeah?"

"Yeah." I leaned down and grabbed Kyla around the waist and took in the scent of her. That beachy coconut smell filled my senses. Her legs came up and wrapped around me. I walked us over to the couch and sat down with her on my lap. She was my constant, my home. This is where she belonged. "You fit everything in that little car of yours?" I teased her.

She smiled down at me. "Sort of. Chris took some stuff in his truck. My furniture is being delivered to the apartment."

I twirled the ends of her hair around my finger. "Chris said you're moving in with him and Tori." I couldn't help thinking about the plans we'd made to live together this fall. That plan fell apart when we did.

Kyla slid off my lap and sat down on the couch next to me. I could tell something was bothering her. "I am," she said. "I really don't know if it's a good idea with them being engaged now, but I really didn't want to live in the dorms by myself." She shrugged her shoulders. "I'm gonna try it for a while, if it feels weird, I'll figure something else out." She threw her hands in the air. "Anyway, it's all good."

I grabbed her right wrist and turned it over. "What's this?" I asked, eyeing the ink on the inside, and tracing the infinity symbol with my finger.

She sighed. "I'm trying new things. I figured since I'm not responsible to anyone but myself, I might as well do what I want. I don't need to seek anyone's approval anymore."

I knew she was talking about her parents, but she was probably talking about me too. I had never meant to hold her back, but maybe I did. I was doing new things too. Maybe we had held each other back. "Well, it looks good. Who did it?"

"I went to this place called Forever Inked. A guy named Zack did it. Offered me a job too. With coming back to school, it wasn't really possible though."

That was strange. "What do you mean he offered you a job? Doing what?"

Kyla sighed. "Designing and drawing tattoos. When he saw the design for this one," she pointed to her shoulder, "he asked to see my portfolio."

I was curious now. I knew Kyla was talented, but I wondered what would make this guy offer her a job. "Let me see."

She pulled up her shirt up, just enough for me to see her shoulder. I ran my hand over it. "It's beautiful, Ky. You drew this?" She nodded her head. I looked at it more closely. The thorns punctured the hearts, dripping blood onto the roses below it. Although it was beautiful, there was something sad about it too. "Want to explain it to me?"

Kyla lowered her shirt, covering the tattoo. "Not really. It's kind of personal. Maybe one day, but not today."

"One day," I repeated. I was a little disappointed, but I had to respect her privacy. There were things I wasn't ready to share with her either.

Kyla quickly switched topics. "So, how's practice going? This is your big year. You've got to be totally stoked."

"I am. The team looks good. It's going to be a great season." I tilted my head at her. "Sure you can't come to the games?"

She took my big hand in her small one. "We've been through this. You know I can't. I need more than you're ready to give. I can't be half in and half out."

I stroked the side of her face. "Then why are you here?"

She closed her eyes and shook her head. "I don't know. It was a bad idea. I was being impulsive. I should go." She stood from the couch and turned to leave.

I reached for her hand and turned her back to me. "Stay. Don't go." I didn't want her to leave. "Stay for a little while."

"Why?" she whispered. "So you can fuck me?"

I pulled her close and spoke softly in her ear. "Do you want me to fuck you?" My dick twitched, making my jeans feel tighter, at the thought of her body under me. I pushed my hardness into her softness, so she could feel what she was doing to me.

Kyla let out a little gasp. "I don't want to want you to. But I do." She turned her head away from me, hiding the emotion on her face.

"Then why are you fighting it? Stay." I begged her.

"I don't want you to think I'm cheap."

I turned her face so I could look her in the eye. "This is us. Me and you. There's nothing cheap about it. We're two consenting adults. We can do whatever we want. It's more than just sex. You know that."

"Is it?"

"You know it is." I wanted to tell her that I loved her, but I couldn't get the words out. "Come on." I led her back to my room and shut the door. I pulled my shirt over my head and walked her to the bed. "I'm gonna take care of you." I pulled her shirt over her head and took in the beauty that was her. I ran my hands down her arms and to her waist. The piercing in her belly button caught my eye. I ran my hand over it. "This is new."

"You like it?"

"It's fucking sexy, is what it is." I kneeled in front of her and ran my tongue over the silver ring. I unbuttoned her shorts and slid them down her legs. She stepped out of them and turned around. On the right side of her lower back was another tattoo. It was a flaming heart that was cracked wide open. Broken. The colors were bright, the flames almost jumped off her skin. It spoke more than her words ever could. I ran my hands over it. The artwork she had put on her body told a story. It was the story of us, even if she wouldn't admit it. "Did you draw this?"

She nodded as she looked over her shoulder. "It's not finished. I'll get the rest of it done when I go home for break."

"I can't wait to see it," I told her truthfully. I undid my jeans, dropping them to the floor and stepping out of them. I stood behind her and ran my hands down her body while kissing her neck. "Kneel on the bed for me." I felt her body shudder as she complied. I leaned over her back, placing soft kisses down her spine, and rubbing my hands over her new ink. Her eyes closed, and her head went back as she arched into my touch.

I unclasped her bra and let it slide down her arms to the bed. I reached around the front of her and took her tits in my hands, gently rolling her nipples between my fingers. I whispered in her ear, "Still want to leave?"

"You know I don't."

I rubbed my dick along her ass. "I want you so bad."

She looked over her shoulder. "Then take me."

I slid her panties down her legs and threw them to the floor. I rubbed my hands over her perfect ass and spread her legs apart. She was glistening wet for me. I ran my fingers down to her pussy and pushed them deep inside her. She let out a loud moan and fell to her elbows. I spread her wetness over her clit and rubbed her sensitive nub. She dropped her head between her arms, her breathing becoming short and fast. I didn't let her come. Yet.

I pushed down my boxer briefs and my dick sprang free. Grabbing her by the hips, I thrust into her pussy. She let out a little yelp as I continued to thrust into her over and over again. She felt so good wrapped around my dick. She pushed her hips back into me and we found the perfect rhythm.

Before I came, I pulled out and flipped her on her back. I kneeled between her legs and licked her pussy up and down. "I love the way you taste, baby."

"Make me come, Ty. Don't tease me." She ran her hands through my hair and pushed me into her clit. I used the tip of my tongue and licked it up and down, then sucked her clit into my mouth. It only took seconds to get her off and then I was inside her. Her pussy clenched my dick as her orgasm took over her body. I thrust into her heat slowly. I started with fucking her and ended up making love to her. She was worth more than a quick fuck and I wanted her to know that. I never wanted her to feel cheap. Not with me. I needed her to know what she meant to me.

I came long and hard. She locked her legs around my waist, and I emptied everything into her. We held each other for a long time, connected as one.

Chapter 31
Kyla

I kissed Tyler goodbye and drove away. Tears filled my eyes, and they began to fall down my cheeks. I didn't even know why I was crying. I knew what it was going to be when I went there. I was so fucking weak. I was disgusted with myself. With how I let him affect me. Why couldn't I just let him go? He was like a drug to me. I got a little taste, and it was never enough. I always wanted more. I needed to be stronger than this.

I got to my new apartment an hour and half later. I parked on the curb and Tori was at the door waiting for me. "What took you so long? I was starting to get worried."

"I made a pit stop," I said. I tried to stop the tears that threatened to fall again, but one fell down my face anyway. "I'm so fucking stupid. It's never going to change, is it?"

Tori hugged me tight. "I don't know, Ky. I don't know why you keep torturing yourself like this."

"Because I still love him." I wiped the tear away. I gave Tori a weak smile. "Help me unpack my car?"

An hour later Tori and I had everything out of my car and into my new room. The furniture had been delivered earlier in the day. I pushed it around until I was satisfied with the arrangement. I started unpacking boxes and bags, putting everything away in the drawers and closet.

In the bottom of the last box was the purple box that held all my memories of Tyler. I cautiously opened it, knowing I was going to regret it. Sitting in the top of the box were the two ultrasound pictures from my pregnancy. I picked up the pictures in one hand and ran the other hand over my stomach. I could feel the emotions I tried to keep at bay, creeping into my chest. I quickly returned the pictures to the bottom of the box and closed it, effectively locking my emotions back away. I found an empty crate, turned it over in front of the closet and stood on it. I placed the box on the highest shelf in the closet toward the back.

I went to the kitchen and made myself a drink, grabbed my drink and the pack of cigarettes from my purse, and walked out to the small patio attached to our apartment. We hadn't bought any patio furniture yet, so I just sat on the cement slab with my legs tucked to my chest. I lit a cigarette and took a long drag. I didn't smoke often, but I had found that it helped to calm me, especially if I was upset or feeling overwhelmed.

My life had changed so much in the last year. Nothing was what I thought it would be. My parents were gone. My baby was gone. And Tyler… well he was basically gone too. I didn't know what we were or what was going to happen. Our baby would have been born by now. I couldn't help but think about what could have been. Now we were basically strangers who fucked occasionally. What the hell was that?

I really needed to get out and make more friends. I depended too much on Tori and Chris. And while they had always been there for me, it wasn't healthy.

I heard the door slide open. "What are you doing?" Tori asked.

"Just decompressing." I held the cigarette up for her to see. I knew that she hated that I started smoking, but she rarely said anything. I think I earned the right to have a smoke once in while if I wanted to. "I'll be in, in a few minutes."

"Do you want to talk?" she asked.

"Not really. I'm evaluating my life. It's kind of a one-person job," I chided.

"Well, let me know if you change your mind." I heard the door slide closed. I dropped my head to my knees. I needed to start taking back control of my life.

The next morning, I woke with a new attitude. I dressed in my yoga pants and sports bra, then pulled my running shoes from my closet. I hadn't gone running in almost a year. I used to enjoy the release it gave me, and I hoped for that feeling again. I threw my hair in a ponytail, stuck my key into my bra, and grabbed my phone. I stuck my earbuds in and scrolled through my music, needing something punishing that would drive me. I finally found what I was looking for and turned the volume up loud. The music blasted into my ears, energizing me. I did some quick stretches and started on my run. I wasn't going to go too far, considering I hadn't run in a long time.

About a half mile into my run, I found my rhythm. My feet pounded the pavement and my muscles burned. I started running harder and faster as anger took over. The sadness had washed away as I realized I was mad. I was mad about the shitty turns my life had taken. I was mad about Tyler cheating on me. I was mad about not being able to tell him about the baby. I was mad about losing my baby. I was mad about my parents leaving me. I was mad about all the responsibility that had been placed on my shoulders. I was mad about packing up the house. I was just mad.

The further I ran and the more my muscles burned, the more the anger faded away. Before I knew it, I was back in front of our apartment. I stretched my muscles out, as the sweat dripped down my face and chest. I took a deep breath and it felt good. I felt lighter, like a weight had been lifted from my chest.

When I came in Tori and Chris were sitting at the table having coffee. I went to the fridge and pulled out a bottle of water. I opened it, drinking half of it in one gulp.

Tori took in my sweat covered body. "You went running?"

"Yep." I drank the rest of the water and threw the bottle in the recycle bin.

"You haven't run in like forever," she said, eyeing me over her coffee cup and raising an eyebrow.

"I know. It felt really good though. It helped clear my head." I grabbed another bottle of water from the fridge. "Chris, can I borrow your truck later? I want to go buy us a patio set, but my car is too small to fit anything."

"Kyla, you don't have to do that. Tori and I can get it," Chris said.

I waved him off. "Consider it a thank you for letting me move in here. I'll go after my shower."

"Okay. The keys are on the hook by the door. Help yourself."

"Thanks. I won't be long I promise." I walked to my room, grabbed some clean clothes, and went to shower.

Later that evening, the three us sat around the new patio table having drinks and talking about their upcoming wedding. They decided to get married next summer after graduation and were so excited. I was happy the two of them were finally going to make it official. Everyone deserved that kind of happiness.

⧗

Two weeks later, we were watching the Michigan State game on TV. It was weird sitting on the couch watching instead of being in the stadium where I usually was. Michigan State was playing Eastern Michigan University. You could tell that the energy in the stadium was through the roof.

Tyler threw pass after pass that put them way in the lead. I knew the game. I had been watching him for years. Every decision he made on the field was expertly planned. My heart swelled with pride after every play. The announcers continued to talk about him being a candidate for the Heisman. When the camera panned to Tyler on the sidelines, I could see him scanning the crowd. I should have been there cheering him on. I couldn't help but feel that I had let him down. He knew why I wasn't there. But still.

I texted him after the game.

Ky: Great game! Congratulations!
Ty: Thanx! Wish you were here! :(

I didn't respond to his text. What could I say to that? The sad face at the end broke my heart.

I decided to surprise him at the next game. The game was at home and then they were on the road for the next two. I asked Tori and Chris if they wanted to go. Chris was all up for it. He and Tyler were still friends, so he was easy. Tori had her reservations. She said I was setting myself up for disappointment. Something inside me told me this was the right thing to do.

We drove separate cars because I didn't know how the night would end. Tyler and I always had the best sex after a game. He was so amped up and he put all his energy into our love making. I had packed a bag so I could spend the night with him.

I wore my Jersey that said JACKSON on the back. I made sure my hair and make-up were perfect. I was ready to win my man back. No more fucking around. We were either going to do this or not. I was going to remind him how good of a team we were. We were meant to be together. I was sure of it.

The game against Wyoming was another blowout. I cheered my heart out for the man I loved. When the game ended, Tori and Chris left. I made my way down to the locker rooms where I always met him after a game. I leaned against the wall in my usual spot. The team groupies were all waiting too. Those skanks would do anything to get one of the guys to fuck them.

I waited patiently. Tyler was always one of the last ones out. I was looking at my phone when someone came up and gave me a great big bear hug, lifting me off the ground. "Hey, girl! I miss seeing you," Cody said as he put me back on the ground.

"Hey, Cody. It's good to see you too."

"Does Ty know you're here?"

I shook my head. "No, it's a surprise. He was disappointed when I said I wouldn't be coming this year. So... here I am."

Cody leaned down close to my ear. "Just so you know... he hasn't been the same without you. He misses you, even if he's too bullheaded to admit it."

"Thanks, Cody. I miss him too. Don't tell him I'm here, okay?"

Cody ran his finger across his mouth, pretending to zip his lips shut. "Mums the word. Go get him."

"I'm gonna try." I smiled. Cody and I gave each other a fist bump and blew it up. He waved over his shoulder and left the stadium.

After another ten minutes, the door to the locker room finally opened again and Tyler walked out. Girls were calling his name, but this was nothing new to me. I stepped forward to make my claim, but what happened next, was not what I expected. Everything changed in a heartbeat.

Tyler threw his arm around a tall brunette and kissed the side of her head. I slowly stepped back into the crowd as they walked off together laughing.

I bumped into something behind me and then I heard her voice. "Looks like you've been replaced, sweetheart." I turned and was face to face with Madison. Even though I had only seen her that one time, I couldn't forget what she looked like. She had a smug smile on her face I wanted to slap off.

"Fuck you, bitch!" I pushed through the crowd toward the exit. When I finally made it out of the stadium, I ran to my car. I leaned against it and slid down 'til I was sitting on the ground. I dropped my head into my hands. I couldn't even cry.

It was a lie. It was all lies. Every word that came out of his mouth was a lie.

He wished I was there. Lie

He missed me. Lie.

He loved me. Lie

He liked to fuck me. Truth.

That's all I was to him. A good fucking lay. If I had not felt cheap before, I certainly did now. I didn't have anyone to blame but myself. I had allowed this to happen. I was so fucking stupid. No more. I was done. I ripped off my jersey and threw it to the ground, leaving it in the parking lot. I got in my car and headed home.

I walked in the door of the apartment and went straight to my room. I changed into my running clothes and headed back out. Tori caught me by the arm in the hallway. She had a look of concern on her face. "Why are you home? What happened?"

"You were right. That's what happened. You've been right all along. I was just fooling myself. He was with another girl."

"I'm sorry."

"Don't be," I snapped. "I'm fucking done."

"Where are you going?" I could hear the worry in her voice.

"Running. I have a lot of energy to burn off."

"It's kind of late. Be careful."

"Don't worry. I'm pissed, not suicidal." I stuck my earbuds in and cranked up the music. Beyonce's "Ring the Alarm", blasted through my ears and I felt a fire inside me that wouldn't go away.

I started running, heading toward the campus. I didn't know exactly where I was going, but it didn't matter. I just kept running. My lungs burned and my muscles ached, but I pushed forward. My mind replayed the whole scene. Me waiting. Him coming out of the locker room. His arm around another girl, kissing her. Madison. *"Looks like you've been replaced, sweetheart."* That fucking bitch started our whole downfall. I hated her. I hated Tyler. I hated the nameless brunette. I fucking hated them all. And most of all, I hated myself for believing all the lies.

When I made it to campus, I stopped running and pulled out my earbuds. I bent over and put my hands on my knees to catch my breath. I shiver ran up my spine and I looked around. It was dark now and there were only a few people walking around. I looked for anything out of the ordinary. I felt like someone was watching me. Nothing seemed off though, it was all in my mind. I was on edge. I pushed the earbuds back into my ears and started back to the apartment. I let the music blast, pushing myself harder and faster. I needed to feel the burn.

By the time I made it back, I was drenched from head to toe. I grabbed a bottle of water and took the bottle of vodka out on the back patio. I downed the water, then took a swig of the vodka right from the bottle. I lit a cigarette and inhaled deeply, letting the tension in my shoulders dissipate. I rested my head in my hand and took a deep breath.

The slider opened and Tori sat down beside me. "You okay?"

I took another swig out of the bottle and another hit off my cigarette. "Not really, but I will be. I knew he had been with other girls but seeing it… gave me a dose of reality I needed. I believed him when he said he loved me. I was so naïve. I believed that he still cared."

"You know what I think?" Tori asked.

I rolled my eyes. "No, but I'm sure you're going to tell me."

"Kyla, I saw him with you after the funeral. He cares. He's just as lost as you are. He's trying to fill the void."

I threw my arms out to my sides. "I'm right here! I've been right here all along! I wasn't enough for him. I've always tried to be there for him. I supported him every step of the way. Yeah, I kept a big secret from him, but he's the one who fucked someone else. He did this to us! I should have ended everything then, but I loved him too much."

"And now?" she questioned.

"And now I love him and hate him. It's a fine line. Part of me will always love him, he was my first and only. But I hate him for what he's done to us. What he's done to me. I deserve better!" I picked up the vodka bottle and downed another shot. "I deserve to be more than a fuck in his long line of whores."

"Wow! That's pretty blunt. Do you really believe that's all you are to him?"

"Hell, I don't know! It's how he's made me feel. Why are you defending him anyway? You're always the one telling me to move on. Warning me away from him."

Tori let out a deep sigh. "I've told you those things to protect you. You two went through some awful shit. Had you not lost the baby, I think you would be together now. You should have seen him at the hospital when we thought we lost you. He told the nurse you were his fiancé. That's how he got to see you. He was a wreck. I'd never seen him cry before that day. He loves you."

"Loved," I corrected, as a tear escaped.

"No... loves. What you guys have comes along once in a lifetime. He's not trying to hurt you. He's trying to deal with the hurt. You two are just dealing with it in different ways. Guys bury their hurt in booze and women. Girls cry their eyes out, watch *Lifetime* movies, and listen to sad music."

"I have done all that, haven't I?"

Tori nodded her head. "Yeah, you have. But my point is, I don't think he's intentionally trying to hurt you."

"Maybe not, but I can't continue this cycle."

"I'm not saying you should. Just think about it before you decide to hate him."

Chapter 32
Tyler

The morning after the Wyoming game I walked Jennifer to the door and said goodbye. I closed the door behind her and leaned against it. I couldn't believe I brought her home last night. I promised myself I was going to quit, but I was so fucking lonely.

Cody stumbled from his room and walked into the kitchen to grab a Gatorade from the fridge. "Damn, I drank too much last night." He unscrewed the cap and washed down a couple of aspirin. "Kyla leave already? I didn't even get to say goodbye. I thought she'd hang around for a bit." Cody sat at the table and hung his head in his hands, nursing his headache. "I like that girl. She's good for you. I'm glad you guys are starting to work things out."

I walked over to the fridge and pulled out a Gatorade for myself. "Kyla wasn't here. That was Jennifer."

Cody's head popped up. "What happened to Kyla? Did you guys have a fight last night?"

I sat down across from Cody, a little confused. I didn't know where this was all coming from. "We didn't have a fight. How do you fight with someone you don't see and hardly talk to?" I almost wished we did have a fight, because that would mean we were actually talking to each other.

Cody shook his head. "Dude, she was at the game last night."

I sat back in the chair and crossed my arms. "No, she wasn't. She said she wasn't coming to the games this year. I've asked her to come. She said she wouldn't."

He pointed at me across the table, and he was pissed. "You're an idiot, you know that? She's the best thing that ever happened to you and you keep fucking her over." Cody got up and started to walk away.

I stood up and threw my arms out. "What the hell are you talking about? What the fuck is your problem?"

Cody turned and stalked back to me. He got right up in my face. "You're my problem. I can't stand watching you treat her like this. She's a great girl. If you're done with Kyla, let her go. Quit stringing her along. I only wish I had someone like her in my life, and you throw her away like yesterday's trash."

"I'm not," I yelled. "We barely talk."

He pushed his finger into my chest. "Then why was she there last night?"

I pushed his finger away. "She wasn't. I wanted her to be, but she wasn't." I was done fighting.

Cody pushed his palms into his eyes. He let out a big breath and rolled his eyes up to the ceiling. "Oh, my God. Dude, she was. I talked to Kyla. She was waiting for you outside the locker room. She was all dolled up, looking cute as can be. She wanted to surprise you."

My eyes went wide as realization hit. I dropped back into the chair. "And she watched me walk away with Jennifer. Fuuuuck! Fucking fuck, fuck, fuck!"

Cody pointed at me. "You fucked up!"

I gave him a hard stare. "You think?"

I ran into my room and grabbed my phone. There were no missed calls or texts. I scrolled to her name and pushed send. It rang and rang. Her voicemail came on "Hi. This is Kyla. Leave a message." I hung up. How do you say, *Sorry for being an asshole* in a message? I dialed again, and it went straight to voicemail. I texted her.

Ty: *Ky, I'm sorry. Please answer your phone.*

I waited a few minutes. Nothing. No response. Shit!

I dialed her number again. Voicemail. "Please pick up, Kyla. We need to talk." I almost said, "I love you," but I didn't.

I texted her again.

Ty: I know you're mad. Please talk to me. Please!

I quickly changed my clothes, grabbed my bike keys and helmet. I needed to clear my head and think. Before I even realized where I was going, I was on the expressway toward Western. My head was spinning. I knew Kyla wanted more. So did I. Why was I being such a stubborn jackass? Why was I so afraid to commit to her? We hurt each other. Then I abandoned her when she needed me most. I kept her at arm's length, when all I wanted to do was wrap my arms around her. I was so stupid and now had probably lost her for good.

She drove all that way just to see me. Shit, I had practically begged her to come. Then when she showed up, I walked away with another chick. I didn't even care about Jennifer. She was convenient. Just another warm body.

Before I knew it, I was stopped at a light by the university. That's when I saw her. She was wearing a sports bra and a pair of running shorts. Her tattoos peeked out from under her clothes and her long blond hair was swinging in a ponytail. Her earbuds were in, and she was running hard, the sweat dripped down her body.

She stopped at the corner and dropped her hands to her knees. She pulled her earbuds out and walked into the coffee shop. I drove my bike around back and parked. I checked my phone one last time, for anything from her. There was still nothing. I set my helmet on the seat and walked around to the front of the coffee shop.

I waited outside for her. A few minutes later she walked out with her Carmel Frappuccino. She wasn't paying attention and walked right into my chest.

"Oh my, God. I'm so…" Then her eyes met mine. "What are you doing here?"

"When did you start running again?" I asked. Her face was flushed and free of makeup. Her tits were pushed up in her sports bra, spilling out the top. I loved her best like this. Natural and beautiful.

She held her cup with both hands. "About a month ago. It's therapeutic. Why are you here?"

"You know why I'm here," I answered.

She started to walk away. "No. I really don't."

I grabbed her arm and turned her around to face me. "You do. We need to talk."

Kyla motioned to a bench around the corner and out of the way. "Don't make a scene." We walked to the bench and sat down. "What is there to talk about?"

"Why didn't you call or text me back?" I asked.

"For what? What's the point? I'm not mad," she insisted.

I put my hand under her chin and looked her in the eyes. "Because I hurt you last night, and I didn't want that to happen. You need to know that."

Kyla took my hand and pushed it away. "I'm not hurt. You want the truth?"

"Always."

"I was mad and hurt. And part of me even hated you." I cringed at her words. "But then I realized this was all on me. I should have never showed up without telling you. I set myself up. I've made it clear to you that I want more. You've made it clear that you don't. I'm the one who can't move on. I'm the one who can't even go on a date without feeling guilty. That's all on me. Not you. I'm the problem."

"You're not the problem. I still…"

"Stop! Don't say it! I've let this go on long enough. I'll always love you, but it's time I love myself more. I'm not mad. I'm not hurt. I'm done! I told you before, I can't be half in and half out. So, I'm out."

"Please don't," I begged. "You know we're good together."

"You're right. We were good together. Not anymore. I needed more. I need more. The sex is phenomenal, but I'll buy a vibrator and get over it. I know you're not having any problems getting your dick off. I'm just one of the many chicks you fuck, and I need to respect myself a little more than that."

I didn't want her to think of herself that way. She'd always been more to me than that. Her words bit into my soul, and they stung. "Kyla, I've been so stupid. I didn't realize what I was doing to you. I want you back. I don't want this to end. You're the only one who matters to me. I'm sorry." I was pleading for her to forgive me. I was shameless. And for the first time in forever, I admitted the truth to myself. I needed her back in my life.

"I'm sorry too." She stood from the bench setting her coffee down. "I'm sorry I wasn't enough for you." She stuck her earbuds in and ran away from me again.

"Kyla!" I yelled. She faded into the distance and never turned back. "You were always enough," I whispered to myself.

Chapter 33
Kyla

I threw myself into my classes. I worked on my portfolio for my internship. I had ignored it the last several months and it was time to get serious. If I wanted a great internship with possibilities for future employment, I needed to put in the time creating both a physical and online portfolio. I started collecting all the work I had done for my classes, including marketing and advertising. I added in the tattoo designs I did for variety. I scanned through my sketchbook and selected a couple to perfect. After looking at all my work, I realized I was well on my way, and this would be easier than I thought.

I hadn't texted or called Tyler in weeks. It was better this way. I needed to stand my ground. I didn't even watch his games on TV, although Chris did. Sometimes when I would walk through to the kitchen, I would glance at the screen, but I refused to sit and watch. The only way to do this was total separation. I felt like I was finally getting to a place where I was happy with me.

He started calling and texting often. I didn't answer any of it. It was difficult for me to blatantly ignore him, but I just kept thinking about that brunette he walked away with. I deserved better. He even sent me flowers. Twice. He hadn't sent me flowers since high school. The arrangements were beautiful, and the cards begged for my forgiveness. They had probably set him back a couple hundred dollars each. It was too little, too late.

It was mid-October and I had just finished my classes for the day. My advisor had looked at my portfolio so far and seemed impressed. I went to my favorite coffee shop to treat myself and review some of my designs. I had a week to pull it all together. I stood in line when someone bumped my hip.

"Long time, no see, pretty girl."

I turned and looked into warm chocolate-brown eyes. I had forgotten how cute he was. "Hey, Jake. How have you been?"

"Good. How about you?"

"I'm actually really good." We moved forward in line. Jake remembered my favorite coffee and ordered for both of us. "Thanks, but you don't have to do that."

"I got it." He took out a few bills and paid the cashier. "Sit with me for a while?"

I nodded, "Sure." We took our coffees and found a table in the corner to sit down. "So, how was your summer?" I asked.

"Great really. I worked with the Chesterfield police department and they're ready to hire me after I get my degree in criminal justice."

"Wow. That's terrific. I'm hoping to get a job in our home area too. Shelby's not that far from Chesterfield. Maybe we'll both end up back in the same area."

"That'd be cool," Jake said. "How was your summer?"

"Not so good." I explained to Jake everything that had happened with my parents. He was sympathetic and kind.

"I'm sorry. That must have been really hard on you," he said.

"It was, but Tori and Chris have been great. They really helped me out. I actually got an apartment with them just off campus."

"Nice." He took a drink of his coffee, staring at me over his cup. "I hate to ask you this but... how's the boyfriend situation? Are you guys on again or off again?"

I let out a little laugh. "Definitely off. I needed to move on. It's over."

Jake got a little smile on his face. His dimples were super cute. "That's good for me," he said. "Maybe now you'll go on a real date with me. How about it? Are you up for it?"

"Yeah, I think I am." This would be really good for me. I needed to get out and I already knew Jake was a great guy.

"What are you doing tomorrow night? Dinner and a movie?"

"Yeah, I'd like that," I said enthusiastically.

"Awesome. I'll pick you up at six?"

"I'll be ready." I winked at him. "I'm looking forward to it."

Jake stood up and pushed in his chair. "Me too. I'll see you at six." He pointed at me and smiled. "Tomorrow night."

I waved goodbye and watched him walk out. I sat back in my chair and smiled to myself. This was good. Really good. I didn't know if anything would become of it, but at least I was getting out there again. I deserved this. Someone who actually wanted to spend time with me.

Jake showed up promptly at six. He was dressed in a pair of jeans and a black button up with the sleeves rolled. His blond hair had that just-fucked look to it. He looked really sexy. Not bad for my first date in four years.

He took me to this cute little French restaurant. We drank wine and had a great dinner. Our conversation flowed naturally, and we laughed a lot. It wasn't awkward at all, in fact it felt kind of wonderful. Toward the end of dinner, he asked me what kind of movie I wanted to see. Definitely not a romance. I was afraid it would remind me of Tyler and kill the mood. Since it was close to Halloween, we decided on a horror movie.

We went to see *The Purge: Anarchy*. It was creepy as hell. Jake put his arm around my shoulders and held me close. I snuggled into his chest, so I could hide my eyes during the scary parts.

Jake brought me home and we parked in front of the apartment building. "Kyla, I had a really great time tonight. You weren't too freaked out by the movie, were you?"

"It was totally freaky, but not so bad with you holding me," I flirted. "I had a good time. Thank you for asking me."

"I would have asked you a long time ago, but you weren't ready. I'm glad you said yes."

I looked down at my hands. "I'm sorry it took so long."

Jake leaned over the console and took my face in his hands. "You're worth the wait." He ran his thumbs over my cheeks. "I'm going to kiss you. If you don't want me to, you need to tell me now."

"I want you to," I whispered. This was my first kiss with someone other than Tyler since high school. I was nervous, but I was ready.

Jake leaned forward and captured my lips with his. It was slow and sensual. Gentle, yet firm. He traced the seam of my lips with his tongue. I opened my mouth and let him in. Our tongues tangled together in a slow dance.

Jake pulled away first. "I should let you go, before I want to go further with you."

I was breathless. "That's probably a good idea."

"Come on, I'll walk you in."

We walked to the door, hand in hand. When we got to the door, I wrapped my arms around his neck. "Thank you for tonight."

Jake wrapped his arms around my waist. "You're very welcome. I want to take you out again."

"I'd like that," I smiled up at him.

Jake leaned down and kissed me again. He was sweet. "I'll call you. Good night, pretty girl."

"Good night, Jake."

He walked back to his car, and I watched him drive away. I opened the door and shut it behind me. I leaned against the door and closed my eyes. I'd made it through my first date in years and I was proud of myself. This was a huge step for me.

Chapter 34
Tyler

I fucked up in a big way. I knew that. It was only a matter of time before Kyla had had enough. I knew what she wanted, and I wouldn't give it to her. I took her for granted. I thought she would always be there. That when I was ready, she would come running back to me. I thought I held all the cards, when really, she did.

I texted and called her several times. She never replied or answered her phone. I even sent her flowers, twice, to say I was sorry. Her silence was killing me. I got what I deserved for toying with her emotions. What killed me the most was her leaving and thinking that she wasn't enough for me. I should have sent her flowers a long time ago.

I quit the girls. The one-night stands. Those girls had come and gone. Not one of them actually cared about me. They just wanted the notoriety of being with the MSU quarterback. Somehow, none of that was appealing to me anymore. It had cost me the most important thing in my life. Kyla.

She never cared about my status or what I could do for her. She wanted to be with me for me. She always supported me. I was the one who didn't support her. I never took her dreams or her talent into consideration. I thought she would always follow me wherever I went. I was so wrong.

Hindsight was a bitch.

I ate, breathed, lived football. If I couldn't have Kyla, at least I had football. I trained harder. I ran faster. I pushed myself. The Heisman Trophy would be awarded in early December. I wanted it. I needed it. At every game, I pushed limits. Instead of going for all the safe plays, I was riskier. Coach would sometimes about have a heart attack, but it always paid off.

We'd been on a winning streak. Our only loss had been to Oregon in early September. Since then, we'd been kicking ass.

We were coming off a victory against University of Michigan, undoubtedly one of our biggest games of the year. Everyone was pumped after that win. We'd had a week off, and tonight we played Ohio State, another huge rival. Same as us, they'd only lost one game so far this season.

The November night air was crisp. Perfect for football. This was our house, under the lights. We didn't let other teams come into our house and push us around. We started the game strong, scoring the first touchdown after a fifteen-yard pass. The Buckeyes tied us up with a touchdown of their own. By the end of the first quarter, we were up fourteen to seven.

Early in the second quarter, Ohio State tied us again. It was a back and forth game. We scored, they scored. At halftime, we were down by seven. Coach was tough on us. He gave us the "get your asses out there and win this game" speech. We'd all heard it before.

In the second half, I just couldn't find the pocket. We ended up settling for a forty-yard field goal. It wasn't enough to tie it up, but it was something. By the fourth quarter they were kicking our ass. I lined up for a long pass, searching for the pocket. And then it happened.

I got blindsided from the left. Being the quarterback, I didn't get tackled often, but when I did, I went down hard. I felt the hit ram into my side, forcing me to the ground. I gripped the ball to my chest, refusing to let go. My right shoulder hit the ground with tremendous force. I felt the bones breaking as the pain seared through my body. My head hit next, bounced up, and smashed back onto the field again.

My last thought before everything went black was, *I guess my dad was right about that degree after all.*

Chapter 35
Kyla

After my first date with Jake, he called me every day. We often met for lunch or coffee. He held my hand and kissed me sweetly. I enjoyed his company. He was interested in me... my talents, my goals, my dreams. It was a nice change.

I knew Jake liked watching the MSU games on TV. I didn't. Most of the games were during the day, so Jake would hang with his friends to watch football, and I would meet up with him afterward.

The night of the Michigan State vs Ohio State game, Jake took me out to a club with some of his friends. There was a dance floor on one side of the bar. On the other side were a few pool tables and TVs, of course tuned in to the game.

We were drinking quite a bit, but the dancing helped to burn off the alcohol. I was feeling good on the dance floor. Jake and I rocked our bodies together. I had my back to his front. His hands were around my hips, and I felt his erection push into my back. Jake and I had only kissed so far, but I knew he was going to want more from me eventually. I didn't know if I was ready for that. To be honest, it scared the shit out of me.

When the music slowed, I turned in his arms to face him. I put one hand on his chest, to give us some space, the other was wrapped around his neck. Jake's arms went around my waist, his hands settled on my ass. I felt a little uncomfortable, but this was how normal couples danced. I was having a good time and I didn't want to ruin it.

After our slow dance, Jake suggested we go hang with his friends for a while. They were over by the pool tables, watching the game. I didn't want to be anywhere near that stupid game, but I agreed for Jake's sake. When we got to the table, he ordered a shot of Jager and a Jack and Coke for himself. I just ordered water. I had a little buzz and didn't want to let it get out of control.

Jake motioned to his lap. "You can sit right here, Ky."

It felt like cold water had been thrown in my face. Nobody called me Ky. Only Tyler. "What did you call me?" I asked.

"I said you can sit here, Ky," Jake repeated.

I tried not to overreact. He didn't know. "Please don't call me Ky. I prefer Kyla. It's just a thing with me."

"Sorry, babe," Jake said sarcastically. "You can sit right here, *Kyla*," he rephrased, putting the emphasis on my name. He pointed again at his lap.

Okay, now he was being a little bit of a dickhead, but I let it go. I pulled up a chair from another table and sat next to him. "It's okay. I'm good," I said.

He looked at me and shook his head. He focused on the game. I focused on my phone. Every once in a while, I would look up at the game, purely out of curiosity. It was the fourth quarter and MSU was losing miserably. Tyler couldn't seem to get the ball where it needed to go. I texted Tori.

Kyla: Sitting here trying not to watch the game. This kind of sucks.

Tori: We're watching too. Sorry your date sucks.

Kyla: It's not that bad… just wish the game wasn't on.

Tori: :(

I looked up at the big screen. I could see Tyler searching the field, looking for someone open. With the ball still in his hands, he was blindsided from the left. I saw him go down and his head bounced off the field. He wasn't moving.

My hands went up to my mouth and I stood. "Oh my, God. Get up! Get up!" Tyler laid on the ground still unmoving. The game had stopped and medical was rushing onto the field. I watched as they worked on him. They took off his helmet and moved him to a stretcher.

I heard the announcer. *"That's a tough break for Jackson. Could be a career ender. He was slated to be a contender for the Heisman Trophy and the number one draft pick at the end of the season. We're still waiting to hear the official report from the field."*

I stood there in shock, waiting to see what would be said next. Jake's eyes were on me as he downed yet another Jack and Coke. "Kyla, sit down. It's just a game. Shit happens." I shot him a death glare. He rolled his eyes at me. "Oh, that's right, he's your ex-lover boy. I thought you were over that fucker."

I didn't know where all the attitude was coming from. Jake had never acted like this before. He had always been nothing but sweet. This was a whole other side of him I hadn't seen before. I was sure it was the alcohol talking. "Just because we're not together, doesn't mean I don't care about his well-being," I answered.

Jake looked back at the screen, taking a large swig of his drink. "Whatever!"

I sat down and texted Tori.

Kyla: OMG. Did you see that? Is he going to be okay?
Tori: Yeah, we were watching. We are on our way there now. Chris wants to go.
Kyla: OK... Let me know what's going on.
Tori: Do you want to come with us?

I thought about that for a moment. I couldn't. I couldn't get sucked back in. I wasn't going to sit in a waiting room with half a dozen other girls like a groupie. I texted her back.

Kyla: No. Just keep me in the loop.
Tori: K... will do.

I sat there staring at the screen in front of me. I waited for any information the announcers would provide about Tyler. The game resumed with a backup quarterback. The game just went on, like nothing had happened. MSU lost forty-nine to thirty-seven. There was no further information about Ty.

Once the game ended, the guys stood from the table. "You 'bout ready to get out of here, babe?" Jake asked. He was slurring a little. Thank goodness we were close to home. I could have taken a cab, but with the turn the night had taken, I didn't want any more conflict.

I smiled sweetly. "Sure. I'm ready when you are."

Jake threw his arm over my shoulder and led me out of the bar. We got in his car, and I buckled my seatbelt. I knew he had been over served, so my senses were on high alert. He took one turn a little fast, but other than that his driving was fine.

When we pulled up in front of our apartment, it was dark. Tori and Chris had already left. Jake got out of the car and walked me to the door. He wrapped his arms around me and pulled me in tight. "Looks like nobody's home. Maybe I could come in?" I could smell the booze on his breath, and I resisted the urge to cringe.

I faked a big yawn. "I'm sorry. I'm super tired. Another night?"

He dropped his arms. "Yeah, another night. I'll talk to you tomorrow?"

I gave him a quick peck on the lips. "Tomorrow for sure. Thanks for tonight."

Jake walked back to his car and left the parking lot. His tires squealed as he made the turn onto the main road. I opened the door and dropped my purse on the table in the entry way. *What the hell was that?*

I went back to my room and changed into sweats. I wasn't really tired. What I was, was worried. I flipped on the television, scanning through the channels until I found *ESPN*. If there was anything about Tyler, this is where I would find it. I watched the replay half a dozen times. Each time I saw it, the knot in my stomach got bigger. There was nothing about how Tyler was, just commentators giving their opinions. One guy thought it was a simple concussion, while another was sure he had broken his arm. I didn't need speculation. I needed facts.

Just after midnight, I realized I was not going to find out anything watching TV. I needed to wait for Tori. She would know what was going on. I decided to text her.

Kyla: Anything yet?
Tori: We're just getting here. I'll let you know.
Kyla: OK... thanx!

I went back to my room and crawled under the covers. This night had been crazy. Jake started out so sweet and then he kind of turned into a jerk. What the hell happened? Was it the alcohol? Jealousy? There was nothing to be jealous of. Yeah, I reacted to the hit Tyler had taken, but so what? We weren't together, but I still cared about him. I would always care about him. Jake would have to deal with that. It's not like I could turn everything off. I was out with Jake, that should have been enough for him. Hopefully tomorrow would be a new day.

I closed my eyes and tried to go to sleep. I kept seeing Tyler getting hit over and over in my head. I heard the announcer's voice, *That's a tough break for Jackson. Could be a career ender.* He had worked so hard for this. I prayed that he would be okay. I fell asleep thinking of the only man that I ever loved.

Chapter 36
Tyler

I woke up and was on my back in a dimly lit room. My head ached and the pain in my shoulder was excruciating. I saw her blond hair pulled back off her face, but I couldn't make out her features. "Kyla?" I whispered in a hoarse voice.

"You're going to be alright." I heard her voice. But it wasn't Kyla's.

"Where's Kyla?" I asked again.

"My name is Emily. We're taking you to University Hospital. We'll be there in a few minutes. How do you feel?"

"My head hurts. My shoulder hurts. Where the hell is Kyla?"

Emily ran her hand down my arm in a soothing manner. "We're still in the ambulance, Tyler. Maybe she'll be at the hospital when we get there. Just relax. We'll be there soon."

I closed my eyes, and the pain took over. And then I was out.

When I woke again, I was in a hospital room. My eyes felt heavy, and my head still ached. I looked down and saw the IV sticking out of my arm.

"Thank God, you're awake," I heard my mom say.

I turned my head to the side and saw my mom and dad sitting next to the bed. My dad ran his hand through his hair. "You scared the shit out of us, son."

"What happened?" I asked.

"You don't remember," my dad questioned.

"A little. I was on the field. I remember getting blindsided and going down. I remember my shoulder cracking on the ground. I remember waking up and I thought Kyla was there, but she wasn't. I don't remember anything else." I looked at my right arm. It was casted from my shoulder down past my wrist. "Fuck! How am I going to play like this?"

My mom and dad gave each other a worried look. "You're not, Tyler. At least not for the rest of this season," my mom said, taking my hand.

"Fuck!" I leaned my head back against the pillow. "How bad is it?" They just looked at me, not sure what to say. "How bad?" I raised my voice.

"Bad," my dad said. "You had some swelling in the brain, but that's gone down…"

I interrupted him, "I don't care about my head. What about my arm?"

My dad blew out a breath. "You have compound fractures in both your clavicle and upper arm. They had to do surgery. They used metal plates and screws to secure the bones and keep them in place."

"So, I'm out! It's over. All that work and it's over just like that! I'm not going to be ready for the draft in April, am I?"

"Let's just see how everything heals, Tyler," my mom said sweetly. "With physical therapy and everything…"

"But not by April. I won't be ready."

My dad shook his head. "No, son, not by the draft. But like your mom started to say, with physical therapy and a personal trainer, you could be a free agent next year. But first we've got to let those bones heal. We'll worry about the rest later."

I looked away from my parents. This all sucked. I was right there. All I had to do was reach out and take it. And now my dreams were shattered just like my shoulder.

I looked back at my mom. "Is Kyla here?"

"I don't know, honey. We've been with you most of the time. There are a lot of people in the waiting room. Want me to go check?"

"Will you, please?"

Mom gave me a little smile. "Sure, honey."

My mom got up and left the room. My dad gave me a quizzical look. "I thought you two weren't together anymore?"

I looked at my dad with regret in my eyes. "I fucked up, Dad."

"What does that mean?" he asked.

"I'll tell you the whole story if you promise not to judge. It's bad."

"You're my son. Nothing can be that bad. I won't judge you."

I rolled my eyes. "You might. I wasn't a very good boyfriend to her." I blew out a breath. "Remember when we went to the Rose Bowl last year?" My dad nodded his head. "Well, when we got back, Kyla was supposed to meet me at the big celebration party. She got stuck in a snowstorm, so she was really late. I started drinking. A lot. I was so hammered, Dad, I could barely see straight. When I thought Kyla got there, I took her up to one of the rooms to…" I paused "…you know?"

"Have sex?" he quirked his eyebrow.

"Yes. Anyway, I was so trashed that all I saw was her long, blond hair. Next thing I knew, Kyla was standing in the doorway watching me. The girl I was with, wasn't Kyla, just some random chick who looked like her."

"Awww shit." My dad ran his hand over his face.

"Yeah, well, she ran out of the party crying. I went the next day to try to work things out with her and we did for a couple of days. Then she ran again. We didn't talk for like six weeks. Then one day she called me, said she wanted to work things out because she missed me. And I was like 'hell yeah' because I missed her too. I was miserable without her." I stopped talking.

"Then what happened? There's obviously more."

"This is the really hard part," I said. "I was on my way to see her, when I got a call from Chris that she was in the hospital and to come there instead. I raced to the hospital. I couldn't lose her, I was just getting her back. When I got to the hospital... I found out she had miscarried."

"She was pregnant," he stated more than asked.

"Yeah, she practically bled out on the bathroom floor in her dorm room."

"Jesus Christ!"

"Dad, I didn't even know she was pregnant. She never told me. She didn't want to mess up my game at the Rose Bowl and then I had cheated on her, so she didn't tell me. She knew I wasn't ready for a baby."

"How far along was she?"

I sucked in a deep breath. "Fourteen weeks." My dad looked up at the ceiling, trying to pull it together. "She said she was going to tell me that night, but then she miscarried, and it was too late. I was so mad at her, Dad. And you know what? She was right. I wasn't ready. I had football and everything, but I would have been there for her. I was so fucking mad." A tear rolled down my face. "And you know what I did? I left her there. I left her in the hospital by herself to deal with everything on her own. I snuck out in the middle of the night like a coward."

"Ty..."

"I was such a jackass. How could I have left her like that? I knew it was hard on her. She really wanted our baby. She was scared and sad. And I just left her alone. And you know what? After I had time to process everything, I realized I wanted our baby too." The tears poured down my cheeks. "I was going to propose to her after the Rose Bowl and then everything got so fucked up. I still have the ring in the back of my dresser."

"You never told me you bought a ring. I knew you two might get married someday. You guys were like two peas in a pod."

I wiped the tears away. "We were good together. I didn't see her again until after her parents' funeral. I wanted to make sure she was okay. She really wasn't, but she's tough, you know? She's handled everything by herself... losing the baby, losing her parents. She wanted me back. I knew she did. And I walked away from her again. Left her alone to deal with things. Right before school started, she came to my apartment. We... we had sex. She wanted more. I wanted her in my life when it was convenient for me. Not how she wanted. I wanted her to be at my games, for me. I was selfish. She said she wouldn't come to the games that it was too hard on her. And then one day she showed up at one of the games, but I didn't know she was there. She watched me walk away with some other girl. Since then, she's cut me off. No texts. No calls. I even sent her flowers. She said she was done. I guess I thought she would just be there when I wanted her. The kicker of the whole thing is... I always wanted her. I still love her. I pushed her away and now she's gone." This was the first time I had really told the whole story to anyone, and replaying it aloud made me realize what a fool I had been.

My dad just sat there for a moment, taking in everything I'd said. "That's quite a story. You two went through a lot. You basically grew into your adult lives together." My dad leaned forward with his arms on his knees. "We never told you, but you know... your mom had a miscarriage when you were little, not even quite two. She wanted another baby so bad, and when she lost it, your mom fell apart. It nearly tore our marriage apart. Losing a baby like that... it's hard stuff. For you and her."

"You're the first person I've told. Only Chris and Tori know."

"So basically, you both went through this on your own. You didn't even lean on each other."

"Yeah, I guess," I said. "I was just so mad at her for not telling me."

"And what if she hadn't miscarried? What do you think would have happened?"

"I don't know. I still would have been mad at first, but we would have worked it out. I think we would be together."

"Do you understand why she didn't tell you?" he asked.

"Yes, I do now. I cheated on her. And I told her I didn't want a baby yet. It wasn't part of my plan." I shook my head. "I didn't make it easy on her."

"Son… plans change. Not everything goes as expected. Just like your shoulder."

"So, what do I do now?"

"About Kyla or your shoulder?"

"Both."

"Are you a quitter? Did I raise you to be a quitter?" he asked.

"No. You never let me quit anything," I said as I wiped at my eyes.

"So why would you quit now? Both will take time. But I think if you work hard enough, you'll figure out how to get both back." My dad put his hand on my knee. "Thank you for sharing everything with me."

"Thanks for listening and not judging me."

"You're my son. I'll always be here for you."

Just then, the door opened, and my mom came back in. "Honey, I didn't see Kyla, but I did find two people who really want to see you." Chris and Tori walked in behind my mom. "We'll give you guys some time alone," she said smiling. My mom took my dad's hand and led him out.

"Hey," I said weakly.

"Hey, tough guy." Tori smiled and sat in the chair next to me.

"Yeah. Not so tough now, am I?"

She winked at me. "I still think you're pretty tough."

"How bad is it?" Chris asked as he sat in the other chair.

"Pretty bad," I answered. "I have compound fractures in both my clavicle and my arm. They put metal plates and screws in me."

"So you're kind of like the bionic man," he teased.

I let out a little laugh. "I guess, but I'm out for the draft. Just like that... gone."

"Sorry, man. That... well, it sucks. What now?" Chris asked.

"Finish my degree. Start physical therapy and try to get my shoulder back." I turned to Tori. "Kyla didn't come with you, did she?"

Tori pressed her lips together and shook her head.

I knew it. She wasn't coming. "She hates me, doesn't she?"

"She doesn't hate you," Tori answered. "She's just really hurt. She blames herself mostly. Kyla's trying to find herself. She's been through a lot."

I turned my head away and stared out the window. "She should hate me. I wasn't there for her when she needed me." I looked back at Tori. "You know what I can't figure out? Why don't you hate me? She's your best friend and I shit on her."

Tori took my hand. "Because you're a good guy, Ty." She leaned over and kissed me on the cheek. "Both of you went through a lot. Neither one of you knew how to deal with it."

"It doesn't excuse how I treated her. I love her and I destroyed her."

Chris piped in, "Give it time, man. She'll come around."

Chris and Tori stayed for quite a while. We talked and laughed. It felt good having my friends back around. It all felt so... normal.

The next several weeks were tough. Cody was a huge help. He helped me with everything. He had to help me take a shower, which was a little humiliating. He drove me to school and even made sure I ate on a regular basis. Chris came up every weekend, to get me out and about. I looked forward to the weekly distraction. I'd ask about Kyla, but all he would say is that she was doing fine. I knew she was dating someone else, and I was glad Chris kept the details to himself.

I was able to keep my scholarship, which was cool. Since I got hurt during a game, and I was their most prized athlete, the school set me up with a tutor. I could barely write my name, let alone take notes or take tests. Luckily, there were only about four weeks left of the semester.

I was bored out of my fucking skull. Going to the games and watching from the sidelines was torture. Every game emphasized to me how much I had lost. But when this cast came off, I was going to work like hell on getting it all back. Kyla included.

Chapter 37
Kyla

Tori and Chris came back the next day and filled me in on Tyler's condition. I was heartbroken for him. I wanted to get in my car and run to him. I wanted to be by his side and help him. But I couldn't. I just couldn't fall back into the same routine. Plus, I'm sure he had plenty of other girls willing to step up and help. I sent him a *get well* card, and called it done.

After my strange date with Jake, everything seemed to go back to normal. He was sweet again, and the guy who I'd seen at the bar didn't return. We spent a lot of time together.

Today he wanted to take me to the shooting range. Jake was going into criminal justice, and he knew how to use a gun, but guns made me nervous. He wanted to try to teach me how to shoot. I said I would try, but really, I had no interest.

We pulled up to the range and Jake pulled his gun bag from the trunk. "You look like a scared rabbit," he said laughing.

"I don't know about this. Guns scare me."

Jake wrapped his arm around my shoulder. "There's nothing to be scared of. It's just a piece of metal. Guns can't hurt you. It's the person holding the gun that is dangerous."

"I guess you're right," I said, as he held the door open for me.

"Just try. If you don't like it, you can just watch me. I have to get in some practice anyway." Jake stepped up to the counter, reserved a lane, and got me protective eye and ear wear.

He put on his own protective gear and led me out to the range. He set the target and sent it out twenty-five feet.

I stepped back. "I'll just watch for a few minutes," I said.

Jake loaded the clip, pulled back the slide, and took aim. He shot off eight rounds in succession. Each time the gun fired, I flinched from the noise. Even with the ear protection it was loud. Every bullet hit toward the center of the target. He was really good.

Jake reloaded and fired again, then waved me over. "Come on. You try."

I stepped up to the lane cautiously. "I don't know about this," I said nervously.

"I'll help you." Jake put the gun in my hand. It felt heavy and awkward. He showed me how to hold it. "Not too tight," he warned. "This thing has a lot of kick, so you need to be ready for it."

I nodded my head. I wasn't totally ready, but I tried my best. I aimed the gun and squeezed the trigger. I shot and my hands jerked up from the force of it. Holy shit!

"Try again," Jake encouraged. "Now you know what to expect."

I aimed again. I held the gun a little tighter and squeezed the trigger. The gun didn't kick as much this time and I was relieved. I hit the target, but it was way off to the side.

"That was better, babe," Jake smiled.

I put the gun down on the counter in front of me. "I think I'm done for today."

"Okay. Well, at least you tried."

It was a pathetic attempt, but this was not in my comfort zone.

"Give me about fifteen minutes and then we'll get out of here."

"Yeah, go ahead. Do your thing."

Jake reloaded the gun several times and emptied each clip into the target. The comfort he felt firing the gun made me uneasy, but this was going to be part of his job, so I guess it made sense.

After the shooting range we went to lunch. "There's a party at one of the frat houses on Saturday. Want to go with me?"

I hadn't been to a party since that night after the Rose Bowl. The night everything changed. I was quiet as I thought about that night. It was stuck in my head, on replay.

"Kyla?" My head jerked up to him. "The party? Want to go with me?"

I forced a smile. "Sure. Why not?" The last place I wanted to go was a frat party, but it was another hurdle I needed to get over.

We finished our lunch and Jake took me back to my apartment. I changed into my running clothes, stuck in my earbuds, and turned on some Kid Rock. After running for the last few months, I was able to run farther and faster. My feet led the way toward campus. I didn't think, I just ran hard and fast. I felt the burn in my lungs and legs. It cleared my head. I didn't want to think about anything. I got to the track and circled it twice, then headed back.

I stopped at a corner and waited for traffic to clear. The tingle I'd had the last few times I'd run, ran down my spine. I always felt like someone was watching me. It was creepy. I looked around and didn't see anything. I needed to get some Mace or pepper spray to carry with me while I ran. I made a mental note to pick some up and continued my run when the light turned green.

My thoughts went to Jake. There was something off about him. I couldn't figure it out. He had been my friend when I really needed one. Our first few dates were really great. He'd been a gentleman the entire time. There was that weird date the night Tyler got hurt, but then everything went back to normal. Red flags were going up. I wasn't sure why though.

I didn't have any experience dating. Things had always been so easy with Tyler. Maybe all of this was normal, and I was making too much of it. I didn't want to go to that party on

Saturday, but I was jaded. It was just a party, right? I'd been to plenty before that night. Why shouldn't I go? I couldn't really think of one solid reason.

Saturday night Jake picked me up promptly at eight. The weather had turned cold. I dressed in my skinny jeans, a cute purple shirt that showed some cleavage, and my tall boots.

"You look really sexy tonight," Jake commented. "I'm going to have to fight the other guys off with the way you look." It was part complimentary, part accusatory.

"I thought I looked nice," I defended.

"You do. Too nice," he said, then gave me a peck on the cheek.

We arrived at the party ten minutes later. We made our way inside and went right to the bar. I had a Captain and diet Coke, while Jake snagged a beer. The place was really crowded, and there wasn't a lot of room to move around. We finished our drinks and made our way to the makeshift dance floor. Jake and I danced for a few songs, rubbing up against each other in a provocative way. His leg was between mine and I teased him, rubbing my core on his leg. I could feel his hardness through his jeans, as we danced dangerously close to one another.

I was getting hot and sweaty. "Let's take a break," I suggested. "I need to get another drink." We walked back to the bar area, and I grabbed another drink. Jake did a lemon drop and offered me one. "No thanks," I declined. Then he made himself a Jack and Coke.

"I'm going to the bathroom. I'll be back in a few," he said.

I nodded. "I'll just wait over here." Jake walked off into the crowd.

"Hey, Kyla."

I turned and saw one of the guys from my marketing class. "Hey, Kevin." I gave him a quick hug and we started talking. I was having a hard time hearing him with all the noise in the room, so I leaned closer to him. He was smart and funny. I was laughing at something he had said when I felt a hand wrap around my arm.

Jake gripped me tightly and pulled me away. "I need to talk to you," he growled. I was roughly dragged through the crowd and out to the patio where it was so cold you could see your breath. Only the smokers were out here, so it was fairly empty. Jake pushed me up against the wall. "What the fuck? I leave you alone for a few minutes and you're hitting on some other guy?"

I pulled back in shock at his words and pushed his hand off my arm. "What are you talking about? We were just talking. It wasn't a big deal," I said. I was offended and pissed.

"It looked like more than just talking. You come here looking like that," he motioned to my outfit, "and then I find you laughing and flirting with some other guy." His brown eyes turned darker, almost black.

"I don't know what you're talking about. He's just a friend," I insisted.

"Yeah, well he looked like he wanted to get in your pants," Jake said angrily.

"You're being ridiculous. We're just friends."

"We've been dating for a while now. If anyone's going to get in your pants, it's going to be me." He pushed me against the wall and pressed his lips to mine, his tongue delving deep inside my mouth.

His possessiveness was both a turn-off and a turn-on. Despite that my mind was telling me to run away, my body responded with need. I felt the wetness pool between my legs. It had been so long since I felt wanted. "Your jealousy will get you nothing. If you want me, you have to treat me right," I responded seductively.

He pulled back. "I'll treat you right. Just give me a chance."

"I am," I whispered.

"Fuck me." It was both an expression of frustration and an invitation.

My head was so conflicted. I had never done anything with anyone but Tyler, but I had needs to be satisfied. And right now, rational thought was being outweighed by need. "What do you want?" I asked. My hormones were going crazy. I didn't even know who I was. The fire in me was going out of control. I needed this.

"I want you," Jake said, leaning in close to my ear.

"Then let's get out of here," I said. I was so turned on. I just needed the relief that I knew he could supply.

Jake led me around the side of the house and out to his car. We drove the few short minutes to his apartment and then we were out of the car. He rushed me inside and to his bedroom. He shut the door behind us and backed me up to the bed. "I've been waiting so long for this," he groaned.

My nerves kicked in as the reality of the situation hit me. It was too late to back out. I had initiated this, now I was nervous as hell. No one, but Tyler, had ever touched me in an intimate way. I had to go through with it, or risk losing Jake, just like I had lost Tyler. He was sexy and had a great body, so what was my problem? I couldn't risk it, so I gave into it. I reached for the bottom hem of my shirt and pulled it over my head.

"Your so fucking beautiful," he said, as I stood there in my bra and jeans.

It was just what I needed to hear. I let go of my inhibitions and gave into the lust that was burning low in my belly. He stripped off his shirt. God, he was built. His muscles bulged and strained with his desire. This was just sex. It didn't have to mean anything. I could do this. I unbuttoned my jeans and slid them down my legs. His jeans came off just as fast.

He pushed me down on the bed and then my bra was off, followed by my panties. He grabbed a condom and put it on. Before I knew it, he was inside me. He thrust hard and fast, searching for his own release. There was no foreplay. I didn't even get a chance to come. He was on top of me, driving in and out like he was possessed. It wasn't gentle. It wasn't intimate. There was no emotion at all. I just laid there and waited for it to be done. I felt him tense up, and then he came. It was over as fast as it had started.

Jake collapsed on top of me, breathing hard. I wrapped my arms around his neck and held him to me so I could hide the disappointment on my face. "That was awesome, babe. Thanks. I needed that," he said.

I pretended like it was good for me too, but all I wanted to do was cry. *Thanks?* He thanked me for sex? This was nothing like being with Tyler. He always made sure I was pleased first. That I was taken care of. Then he would make love to me. I guess that was the difference. This was just fucking, not making love.

Jake got up, threw the condom away, and started getting dressed. That was my cue. I rolled to the side of the bed and searched for my clothes. I quickly got dressed and tried to keep the tears out of my eyes. I was thankful it was dark so Jake couldn't see my face.

"You want to go back to the party?" Jake asked. I was just a quick fuck. An intermission of sorts.

"You can, but I'm kind of tired. Would you mind taking me home first?" I asked.

"Sure. No problem." His tone told me he didn't care one way or the other.

I was quiet on the ride home. I was too far inside my own head. Jake walked me to the door. "Tonight, was really great," he said, as he hugged me goodbye. "I'll call you tomorrow." I just stood there and watched as he jogged back to his car.

I opened the door and hurried straight to my room. I stripped out of my clothes and went to take a shower. I felt dirty. Cheap. Used. I stepped into the scalding water and let the shame wash away. What the fuck had I just done? I let him fuck me, and what did I get out of it? Nothing.

I took the shower head off the wall and aimed it at my most sensitive parts that still hadn't had any relief. I let the water pulse against my clit and moved the shower head back and forth. I felt the sensation begin to build low in my sex. I squeezed my thighs together over and over as the feeling began to increase. I could feel it building and I couldn't stop. When it reached its peak, I let go and let the pleasure wash over me. I dropped my head back. Finally! I was ashamed that I had resorted to this. Pleasing myself was a sad replacement for Tyler's tongue, but a girl had to do, what a girl had to do.

Chapter 38
Tyler

My dad had done some research and found one of the best orthopedic doctors for sports injuries. Dr. Browning's office was close to home, which worked out perfectly. Since the semester was over, my mom and dad came up to MSU to pick me up and bring me home for the holiday break. I insisted we bring my car home, because as soon as the cast came off, I wanted the freedom of driving. Even though Cody and the other guys from the team had been great about giving me rides, I hated depending on other people.

My dad drove my car home and I rode with mom. She asked about how school was and how I had been managing with my arm being casted. Even though the conversation was light, the tension in the car was heavy. "Did dad talk to you?" I asked.

My mom laughed. "Your dad talks to me all the time. You'll have to be a little more specific than that."

"About what happened between me and Kyla?"

She looked over at me then turned forward again. "He did."

"Are you mad at me?" I asked.

"No." She shook her head.

"Disappointed?" I tried again.

"Sweetheart, stuff happens. I'm not disappointed. Want to talk about it?" she asked.

I looked out the side window. "I don't know." I had questions I needed to ask her, but I knew that I might be pushing across a line with her. "Dad said you had a miscarriage when I was little."

I saw my mom's hand tighten on the steering wheel and she swallowed the lump in her throat. "I did," she said.

"How did you deal with it? I mean, how did you get over it? I guess I'm trying to figure out what Kyla was thinking. How she was feeling."

My mom let out a big sigh. "She was probably scared to death. It's one thing to get pregnant when you're trying. It's a whole other thing when you don't know how the other person feels. I'm sure she was scared to tell you because you two are so young and weren't planning on it."

"She was scared. I knew she was scared," I said. "When she lost the baby, she was so sad. I didn't care about the baby at the time. I just wanted her to be okay, but she… she acted like a crazy person in the hospital. She… I don't know… I had never seen her act like that before."

"Tyler, think about it. She carried that baby for… how long?"

"Fourteen weeks."

"That's three and a half months. It was part of her. She watched her body grow and change. She probably saw pictures of it and heard its heartbeat. When you hear the heartbeat, you can't help but fall in love with the tiny person growing inside you." A tear ran down my mom's cheek and she quickly wiped it away.

"I'm sorry, Mom. I shouldn't have asked about this."

"No, it okay. I'm glad we're talking about it."

"How did you deal with?" I asked.

"Honey, I was a mess. I didn't eat for days. I couldn't sleep. All I could think about was the baby. Your dad tried to help me snap out of it, but he really didn't understand. I don't think a man can ever really understand how a woman feels when something like that happens. But he tried, and I can't fault him for that."

"I didn't even try to help her. I just walked away. What does that say about me?"

My mom patted my knee. "You were young and in shock, I'm sure. It doesn't make you a bad person."

"Maybe. I'm not so sure I agree with you. How long was it until you got over losing the baby?"

"That's a tough question… the initial pain fades after a few months. But getting over it? I'm not sure a woman ever does. Even today, when I see a pregnant woman or a newborn, my mind goes back to losing my own baby. I still get sad sometimes. It never really goes away." Another tear fell down her cheek and she just let it roll down off the side of her face. "But you know what? I was lucky enough to have one perfect son. And that's enough for me." Mom reached over and squeezed my hand.

I squeezed her hand back. "I'm far from perfect, Mom."

"Oh, Tyler. Your perfectly imperfect. I'm proud every day that you're my son."

"How do I get her back, Mom? I miss Kyla so much. I love her."

"You know your dad and I love her too, right? She's like a daughter to me. She's lost everything in a very short amount of time. You're coming home to spend Christmas with your dad and me. Who is she going to spend Christmas with? She lost you, the baby, and her parents. She's going to be alone and that just breaks my heart. Start thinking about what she needs and then be that for her."

"That's going to be hard to do when she won't even talk to me."

"It's going to take time, that's for sure. But keep at it. I think she's worth the effort." Mom turned and gave me a smile.

"She is," I said.

A few days after getting home, dad took me to see Dr. Browning. He used a saw to cut the cast off. It was such a relief to have that heavy thing off my arm and to be able to actually move it. After some x-rays, Dr. Browning decided it was healing really well, and that it wouldn't need to be re-casted. He fit me with a special brace and sling. He said that it was important that I keep the brace on as much as possible, but I could take it off to shower. He also gave me the okay to drive. Thank goodness!

I needed to come back to see Dr. Browning in a month. Depending on how everything looked, I would be able to start physical therapy. He was able to recommend a therapist close to MSU that specialized in sports injuries. He warned me that the therapy would be very painful at first, but to stick with it if I ever wanted to play football again. I was going to play football again. It wasn't even a question. I had a little over a year to be ready as a free agent.

Chris and Tori came home for Christmas. They were going to work on planning their wedding while they were here. The wedding was this upcoming summer.

Chris and I met at the bar for lunch. He was already sitting at a table when I got there and had ordered me a beer. He stood as I walked over and gave me bro hug. He pointed at my arm. "The cast is gone. How does it feel?"

"It's still sore, but that cast felt like an anchor weighing me down. I still have to wear this brace, but at least I can move it now. And drive and shower by myself and write my own fucking name. That thing was a pain in the ass." I took a long drink of my beer. That was something else I missed. No alcohol while I was on the pain killers. I rarely needed them anymore and this was my first beer in over a month. It tasted like heaven as it slid down my throat.

"I'm glad we're having lunch. Tori's had me running all over trying to plan this wedding. She wants to have it at the Grosse Pointe War Memorial. It's kind of pricey, but it's what she really wants, so I can hardly say no. We've looked at cakes, DJs, invitations… like I give a fuck what kind of paper the invitations are on." Chris downed the last of his beer and motioned to the waitress to bring us two more. "It makes Tori happy though, so I need to at least pretend I'm interested."

"That's love, man." I laughed. "What's she doing today?"

"She and Kyla are out looking at dresses. I'm finally getting a day off."

I picked at the label on my bottle. "Is Kyla staying with you guys for Christmas?" Chris and I usually didn't talk about her, but I wanted to know what she was doing.

Chris shook his head. "Nah. We asked her to, but she wouldn't. She came back with us at Thanksgiving, but I think she felt like she was intruding. She's just here to do the dress thing with Tori and then she's going back to the apartment."

"Alone?" I asked. "She can't spend Christmas alone."

Chris shrugged. "We tried, but she didn't want to stay."

"She's a stubborn one for sure, but it makes me sad for her. Is she still dating that guy?" I questioned.

"Yeah." Chris rolled his eyes.

"You don't seem impressed," I noted. "What's the story?" I didn't want to hear about her with some other guy, but my curiosity got the best of me.

"You sure you want to hear about it?" Chris asked.

I took another swig of my beer. "Not really, but I need to know. I want her back. I need to know what the competition is like. What's wrong with him? Why don't you like him?"

Chris leaned forward with his arms on the table. "I don't know, man. Nothing's really wrong with him. We've watched football together a few times. He was cool, but…" He got a weird look on his face.

"But what?" I prodded.

"There's just something about him that makes me uneasy. He's nice. He's good-looking." I rolled my eyes. "Seems to really be into her, but I get a vibe from him I don't like. Sometimes he looks at Kyla like she's more of a possession than a girlfriend."

"Has she slept with him?" I asked.

"That... I don't know. If I had to guess... I'd say yes."

Fuck! I didn't want to hear this. "Is she happy?"

"Happy is a relative term with her. Is she happy like she was with you? No... not at all. But she's trying to be. She's searching for something in her life to be good."

I sat there picking more of the label off my bottle. "She deserves something good in her life. I just want her to be happy. It'd be better if she was happy with me, but... whatever."

Chris got a devilish look on his face. "I think I know of a way to give her a little push in your direction. It's not for a few months but... I was going ask you anyway."

I was feeling defeated. "What's that?" I asked. I was hardly listening to Chris. I was thinking about my girl.

"Will you be my best man at the wedding?"

That snapped me out of it. I couldn't stop the smile from my face. "I'd love to! But wait... what about your brother?"

"He's four years older than me. We're not that close anymore. He's starting a family and everything. I really want it to be you."

"Dude, I'd be honored. I can't believe you're getting married this summer." I raised my bottle to his and we clinked them together. I lifted my bottle to my lips and was about to take a sip when I realized what was going on. I tipped the bottle in Chris's direction. "Kyla's going to be the maid of honor, isn't she?"

"Yep! She won't be able to avoid you at the wedding. She's going to be forced to spend time with you."

I shook my head. "It's a bad idea. She's going to have a fit when she finds out."

"It's not a bad idea. It's genius. Besides, it's my wedding, she doesn't get a say."

I let out a big breath. "I just hope your wedding doesn't become my funeral."

Chapter 39
Kyla

Tori stood in front of the mirror in the fourth dress she tried on. "I don't know," she said. "It's pretty and all, but I don't think it's the one." She smoothed out the bottom with her hands and turned to the side to see the back.

"It's beautiful, but I agree, it's not the one," I said. I handed her another dress. "Here, try this one on."

Tori talked to me through the curtain of the dressing room. "After we find my dress, we'll have to find one for you. You're going to be my maid of honor, right?"

I sat in the chair picking at my nails while she changed. Tori hadn't officially asked, but I had assumed she would ask me. "Of course. Who's the best man? Chris's brother?"

Tori was silent for a second. "Nope."

I looked up at the curtain. "Then who?"

"Don't worry. It's someone you know."

I scrunched up my eyebrows while thinking. "Who?"

Tori pulled back the curtain a bit and popped her head out. "Tyler." Then she quickly pulled the curtain closed again.

My eyes popped open. *What?* I jumped up and pulled the curtain back. "You can't be serious?"

Tori put her hands on her hips. "Get in here and close the curtain." I closed the curtain and gave her a stern look. "I am serious and you're going to do it because you're my best friend. It won't be that bad. You walk down the aisle, dance together… simple."

I let out a huff. "Jake's gonna love this," I said sarcastically.

"Who cares what he thinks? You two might not even be together by then."

I sat on the bench in the dressing room. "True." Tori slipped into the dress I had handed her. "Can I ask you a personal question?"

"Of course." Tori turned her back to me. "Zip me up?"

I carefully zipped up the back of the dress. "What's sex like with Chris?"

She turned back to face me. "Okay, that is a little personal. Why do you ask?"

I shrugged my shoulders and tears welled in my eyes. "It's just that Tyler was so… attentive. He always made sure I was taken care of first. It was always so good. But he's the only one I have to compare to. I don't know if that's normal." I wiped the tears away. "I slept with Jake. It wasn't the same. It was more like wham, bam, thank you ma'am. There was no connection. I didn't feel satisfied after… I felt kind of dirty. So, I tried it again a couple of times, but nothing's changed. I just don't know what's normal." I snuffed my nose and wiped at my eyes. "I feel stupid asking you about this."

Tori kneeled in front of me and took my hands. "Oh, Kyla… if he doesn't make your heart pitter-patter, why are you with him? Has he even made you come once?"

I shook my head. "What's wrong with me?" The tears ran down my face.

Tori wrapped her arms around my shoulders, and I hugged her tight. "Nothing's wrong with you. You're beautiful, smart, sexy. You deserve better. You need to end it with Jake."

"Then I'll be alone again," I cried.

"Better alone than with someone who doesn't care about your needs." Tori stood and looked in the mirror.

I wiped my eyes again and pointed at her dress. "That's the one."

I had one more thing to do before I headed back to Western. I stopped by to see Zack. I needed him to finish the tattoo on my back.

"Hey, Kyla," Zack said, when I walked through the door. "You ready for me to finish that tattoo for you?"

"Yep, I finished drawing it up." I handed him my design.

"Damn, girl. This is beautiful. You really do have talent." He motioned for me to follow him to the back. "When you come back this summer, come see me. We'll work something out. My clients would love your designs, especially the ladies. Your stuff has such a feminine look, they'd sell like crazy. I'd pay you a commission for each one I sold."

I laid down on the table. "I'll definitely think about it. It would be nice to make some extra cash."

Zack went to work making the transfer and placed it on my back and up around the side. "How's that look?"

"It's perfect."

"Okay this is how were going to do this. I'll start down here on your back, then I'll need you to turn on your side." He ran his finger up under my right breast. "When we get up here, you'll have to take your bra off, but I'll give you a drape to cover yourself. You cool with that?"

"Yeah, that's cool," I said. Zack was totally professional and never made me feel weird about having my body exposed.

"Okay, let's get this started." Zack put on his gloves and the tattoo gun buzzed to life.

It took Zack five hours to complete my tattoo. I knew the design was intricate and it would take a while, so I wasn't surprised. Zack talked to me the whole time and I explained the meaning of my tattoos to him. He was a good listener and a really nice guy. He wiped the last of the ink off my body. "All done, sweetie. Ready to see it?"

"How's it look?" I asked.

"Almost as beautiful as you," he said with a smile.

"Are you flirting with me, Zack?" I asked with a little laugh.

"Hey, can't fault a guy for trying." He motioned to the mirror. "Come on, take a look."

I looked in the mirror and almost started crying. "Oh my God, Zack! It is beautiful!" It was a series of four butterflies. The first was coming out of the flaming broken heart I'd had done previously. The butterflies wound up my side, each one with its wings a little further opened. The last one sat on my ribcage right underneath my right breast. Its wings were spread wide open, ready for flight. The designs on the butterflies were intricate and the colors vibrant. This was my story. My past and my future rolled into one beautiful piece of artwork. I wasn't quite to the last butterfly yet, ready to take flight and be free, but I was working on it.

"Told you so," he said as he crossed his arms over his chest, looking pleased with himself.

I turned and launched myself into his arms. "Thank you!" I gave him a chaste kiss on the cheek.

"You're welcome," he said hugging me back. "Let's get you bandaged up."

I left feeling really happy for the first time in what seemed like forever. I promised Zack I would come back when school ended, and we'd talk more about his offer.

The drive back to Western was long and a light snow started falling just in time for Christmas. It was late and dark by the time I arrived at the apartment. Our parking lot was practically empty. Most of these apartments were rented by college students and almost everyone went home over break. I was the exception.

As I was sticking my key in the door, I heard an engine rev out in the parking lot. I turned to see what it was, but it was so dark I could barely see anything. Headlights flashed in my face twice, practically blinding me. Then the car roared to life, speeding out of the parking. The car fishtailed on the slick road. "Jerk!"

I let myself into the apartment and carried my bag to my room. I flipped on the light and set my bag on the bed. My room smelled like my body spray. The coconut scent filled my senses. It was kind of strong, but maybe it always smelled like that, and I was noticing it because I'd been away for a few days. I'd have to ask Tori about it. If it smelled like this all the time, I'd seriously have to cut back on the spray.

I started to empty my bag so I could put my dirty clothes in the hamper. Tomorrow would be laundry day. I picked up the pile of clothes and went to drop them in the basket. Sitting on the floor outside the hamper was one of my black thongs. I picked it up and threw it in with the rest of my clothes. I was usually better than that about leaving my underwear on the floor. Chris came in here frequently and he didn't need to see my unmentionables.

I finished unpacking and putting everything away. I went to the kitchen to make myself a drink and carried it to the couch. Christmas was still two days away, so there were a ton of *Lifetime* movies on. I turned on the TV and was happy to see one of my favorites was on, *Holiday in Handcuffs*. It was a little cheesy, but Mario Lopez was such a cutie. I pulled a blanket off the back of the couch and cuddled up.

About a half hour later, my phone buzzed. It was a text from Jake.

Jake: *Still coming home tomorrow? I miss you. Call me when you get in.*

I set my phone back on the end table. I would just let him think I wasn't back yet.

He was another issue I needed to deal with. Tori was right. Why was I wasting time with someone that didn't make my heart flutter? He was getting a little clingy, to be honest. He would call several times during the day just to see what I was doing. He showed up after my classes to walk me wherever I happened to be going. God, he was everywhere. I was starting to feel like I had a shadow. At first, I thought it was sweet, now it was just becoming annoying.

He was definitely good looking and had a great body, but something was missing. The kissing was good. Passionate, possessive, urgent. But the sex really did suck. Maybe I was spoiled from the way Tyler had pleased me, but Jake didn't even try. He went right for the kill every time. Most of the time I laid there like a dead fish, waiting for it to be over. Jake didn't seem to even notice. He was too busy getting himself off.

The next morning, I decided to get up and go for a run. It was cold out, but tolerable. I put on my Under Armour, then a pair of sweats and a thick sweatshirt. I knew I would be drenched by the time I got back with all these clothes on, but I didn't want to get sick either. I grabbed my phone and earbuds and started on my usual route.

It was deserted around campus. Everyone had gone home, plus it was so damn cold out, anyone who'd stuck around was surely inside where it was warm. I stopped at my favorite coffee place on the way back just to warm up a little bit. I sat at a table and scrolled through my phone while I drank my coffee. I had a missed call and two more texts from Jake.

Jake: Are you back yet?
Jake: Call me when you get home.

Jeez! Impatient much. I exited out of the texts and decided to take a look at my online portfolio. It had turned out excellent, if I did say so myself. I needed to have Tori take a picture of my new tattoo so I could add it next to the drawing on my site. My professor loved my portfolio and found me a great internship that I would start in a couple of weeks. If all went well, they would offer me a job after the internship. I was excited because this company had a few locations, and one was close to home. And with the internet, sometimes you didn't even have to meet with the actual clients. Everything was done using the computer. This job, if I got it, would provide me the freedom and range of clientele I wanted to make a name for myself.

I finished my coffee and started back toward the apartment. When I got closer, I saw Jake's car in the parking lot. Fuck! It was definitely time to get rid of him. I stuck my phone in the pocket of my sweatshirt and ran up to his car. I tapped on the window to get his attention. He got out of the car with a bouquet of flowers. Well, maybe today wasn't the day to break it off. He did bring me flowers.

"Hey, babe. Did you get my messages?"

"No. Actually, my phone died." I walked us up to the door and let us in, pulling off my sweatshirt.

"Did you get home this morning?" he asked suspiciously.

"Yeah," I lied again. "I decided to go for a run before I showered. I was going to call you after that." I took the flowers from his hands. "Thanks. These are really pretty." I gave him a quick kiss and walked into the kitchen to put them in some water.

"Well, I happened to drive by and saw your car. When you didn't answer, I decided to wait for you. I was starting to get worried because you didn't call or text."

Happened to drive by? With flowers? This really wasn't that close to his apartment. "I told you my phone died," I explained again.

"Yeah, I know. I'm just glad you're okay."

"I'm fine," I assured him. "Listen, I really need to take a shower. Make yourself at home and I'll be out in a few." I smiled sweetly but thought to myself *or you could leave.*

I grabbed my clothes and jumped in the shower. I washed away the sweat and grime, careful of my new tattoo. I spent a little extra time pleasing myself with the showerhead. I had begun doing that more and more often. It was pathetic, but someone had to make me feel good and it sure as hell wasn't Jake. After I got myself off, I turned off the shower and wrapped a towel around my body. I threw on some comfy clothes and went to find Jake.

He was sitting on my bed looking through my sketch book. Why was he in my room? "Hey, babe," he said when he saw me. "These are really good."

"Thanks." I picked up the ointment off my dresser. "Can you help me put this on," I asked holding up the tube. "It's kind of hard to reach back here." I pulled up my shirt so he could see my new artwork.

"You got another tattoo?" Jake furrowed his eyes. "Don't you think you have enough?"

"It's not really another one," I stated, pointing to my back. "This one wasn't finished. So yeah, it's new, but not a new concept. Now it's complete."

Jake grabbed the ointment from my hand. "Whatever you say." He started spreading the ointment over the lower butterflies and worked his way up. "How far up do these things go? Fuck, Kyla! Did you let him feel you up? It's practically on the bottom of your tit." Jake's voice was irritated.

"No," I said, feeling irritated too. I took the ointment out of Jake's hand and finished doing it myself. "Zack is professional. He wasn't looking to cop a feel." I pulled my shirt back down.

"I don't believe that. I don't like other guys touching you. How about you lay off the tattooing? That guy doesn't need to be touching your tits or anything else."

"I don't plan on getting anything else. Why don't you just drop it?" I turned and walked to the front room and flicked on the TV. *What the hell?*

Jake followed me out and plopped down next to me on the couch. "Don't get pissed because I don't want other guys touching you." He acted like I was the one being unreasonable.

"I said I was done. Let it go."

"Fine. I gotta go to work. I'll call you later. Maybe we can watch a movie or something?"

"Yeah, okay," I said dismissively.

Jake walked out the door in a huff. I really needed to end this.

I went out later to buy a few Christmas decorations. Since Tori and Chris went home and they expected I would go with them, we hadn't decorated the apartment at all. Christmas was one of my mom's favorite times of the year. Our house was always full-out decorated with trees, lights, wreaths, ribbons, and bows. It didn't seem right that I didn't do a little something.

The stores were practically cleaned out of decorations, but I did find a few strings of colored lights and a wreath for the door. When I got home, I hung the wreath with some fancy over-the-door hook I bought. I found a package of pins I had, then pulled one of the chairs from the kitchen into my room to stand on. I started pushing the pins into the wall and hung the lights around the top of my room. It took a while, because I had to pound most of the pins in with one of my shoes. When I finished, I stood back and looked at my handiwork. Not bad. At least now I had a little bit of Christmas spirit.

Jake was planning on leaving tomorrow for home. He wanted to get there in time for Christmas Eve dinner. He didn't even invite me, which I thought was kind of rude since he was my boyfriend, but whatever. It was a relief he hadn't asked. Chris and Tori wanted me to stay back home with them, but I felt like a third wheel. Thanksgiving was nice, but they needed to be able to do things without worrying about me. Besides, Tori would be dragging Chris all over town trying to get things done for the wedding.

Nope, I was resigned to being by myself. It would be like any other day except I would probably watch a marathon of Christmas movies. Maybe I could order some Chinese food. That would be so cliché. I giggled, as I thought about the movie *The Christmas Story*. "Fa-ra-ra-ra-ra ra-ra ra-ra," I sang to myself.

Jake came over later that night, just like he promised. I wished he hadn't. We were sitting on the couch watching TV. Jake had his arm around my shoulder, pulling me into his side, when I realized I couldn't do this anymore. It was time!

I picked up the remote and turned the TV off. "Hey, I was watching that."

I moved to the other side of the couch and leaned against the arm rest. "Jake, we need to talk."

"Can it wait? I was really into that movie?" His voice was laced with irritation.

"No, it really can't," I insisted.

"Fine! What do you want to talk about?"

I took a deep breath. "I think we should break up," I blurted out.

His head flipped around to look at me. I had his attention now. "What? Why?"

"I'm just... I'm not really feeling it. You're a really sweet guy and everything, I just don't feel like we have a romantic connection. I think we were better as friends." *And you're clingy and annoying the shit out of me.*

"Wow! I didn't see that coming," he said. "Is this about the ex-boyfriend?"

"Tyler? No. I haven't talked to him since before we ever started dating. I told you that was long done. This is about me. I'm going to be starting my internship and I really need to focus on that."

"Well, I am surprised, but I understand. Thanks for being honest about it. Would it be okay if I called you next week sometime and maybe we can go for coffee?" he asked.

I gave him a warm smile. This was going better than I expected. "I'd like that. We can still be friends."

"Friends it is," he said. Jake came over and gave me a big hug. "I'll call you next week." He started walking toward the door.

"Sounds good. Have fun with your family this week." I opened the door for him, and he was gone. I watched him drive off and then shut the door. *That was easy!* I was amazed at how well he had taken that. I was expecting him to be angry and throw a fit. It was almost too easy.

I slept in the next morning, Christmas Eve, and was awoken by someone knocking on the door. Who would be at the door at—I looked at the clock—10:30 in the morning? I stumbled to the door and looked out the peephole. A delivery guy was standing on the other side.

I opened the door in all my morning beauty, hair a mess and makeup smudged under my eyes. "Kyla," he looked at his clipboard, "O'Malley?"

"That's me," I answered.

"I have a delivery for you. I need you to sign for it." He pushed his clipboard at me. I took the clipboard, signed on the line, and handed it back to him. He handed me two boxes. One was quite large and looked like it might be from a florist. The other was small, wrapped in plain brown paper. "Have a good holiday," he said and left.

My heart sank. This was probably from Jake. He was going to make this breakup harder than it needed to be. I took both boxes over to the kitchen table.

I decided to open the big box first. I clipped the straps holding the box together and pulled off the top. It was an absolutely gorgeous arrangement of red and white roses. There was a card attached. I pulled it out and read it. *Hope this brightens your day. I'm thinking of you! All my Love~ Tyler* My heart pitter-pattered in my chest for the first time in a what seemed like forever.

I set the card down, reached for the smaller box, and pulled off the brown paper. The box was wrapped in a pretty silver foil. I carefully pulled the foil off and set the box on the table. It was a plain black box. I don't know why, but I was nervous to open it. *Just do it!* I told myself. I hesitantly picked up the box and lifted the lid. Sitting inside the velvet-lined box was a silver pendant, shaped as two hearts connected together by the infinity symbol, surrounded by…diamonds? I carefully took it out of the box and placed it around my neck. I went to the bathroom and looked in the mirror. It was gorgeous, and if I had to guess… expensive. I lifted it off my chest, ran my fingers over it, then pressed it back against my chest. I looked at the inside of my wrist. Surely my infinity symbol had been his inspiration.

I went to the kitchen and took the note out of the box. *You still have my heart. Please give me another chance. I Love You! ~Tyler* I stared at the note and started to cry. Just when I thought I was over him, he had to go and do something like this. Okay, I would never really be over him, but still.

I took the necklace off and set it back in the box. I didn't even know how to respond to this. I couldn't ignore it like the flowers he had sent before. A simple text saying *thank you* didn't seem appropriate. But if I called him, I would get sucked right back in. Should I even accept this gift? If I didn't, it would crush him. Maybe a thank you note would be better. I would really have to think about what to do.

I left everything on the kitchen table and went off to take a shower and think.

I got out of the shower and threw on a pair of pajama pants and a tank top since I had nowhere to go today. I was towel drying my hair when there was another knock at the door. I looked through the peephole. Jake. I would have thought he had already left to go home for Christmas Eve dinner.

I opened the door and Jake pushed his way in. "What are you doing here?" I asked as I shut the door behind him. "I thought you were going home."

He stood with his hands on his hips and a scowl on his face. "I am," he said. "But I needed to take care of something first. I changed my mind."

"Changed your mind about what?"

"Us!" he shouted. I took a step back. "I'm not just going to be your friend!"

I tried to look brave, but the anger that was radiating off him scared me. "I'm sorry you feel that way. But it's over."

He took two long strides until he was right in front of me. He towered over me, looking down with hate. Instead of being brown, his eyes looked black as coal. Then he grabbed my arms roughly and nearly picked me up off the floor. "The fuck it is! It's over when I say it's over. You're mine now and I'm not letting you go!" He dragged me into the kitchen and threw me into one of the chairs.

He looked at the flowers and necklace on the table. "What the fuck is this?" He picked up the card from the flowers and read it. "I thought you said this wasn't about him. You're a fucking liar!" He threw the card back on the table, picked up the vase, and threw it against the wall. The crystal vase smashed into a million pieces. The flowers fell to the floor and water dripped down the wall. The necklace followed, flying through the air.

I cowered down into the chair. "Stop! Just stop!" I yelled.

"I'll stop when you stop fucking lying! You lied to me yesterday too! You didn't get home in the morning! You got home the night before! I fucking saw you! I was here! What else are you fucking lying about?"

The tears started to run down my cheeks. "I was tired when I got home."

"I bet your phone didn't die either, did it?" I just stared at him. "Did it?" I flinched back into the chair.

"You're scaring me," I whimpered.

"Good! You should be scared! You're fucking mine!" He grabbed me hard by the arm and yanked me up out of the chair. "As a matter of fact, I'm going to show you just how much you are mine!"

"Stop! Please! What are you doing?" I screamed. He ignored my screams as he dragged me back to my bedroom. "No, no, no, no! Please don't!" I tried to dig my heels into the carpet, but it was no use. He was too strong! The tears poured down my face. I pounded my other fist against him, but he wouldn't let go. "Stop! Just stop! Jake, don't do this!"

He pulled me into the bedroom, picked me up and threw me on the bed. I tried to scramble away from him, but there was nowhere to run. I was trapped. His body blocked the only way out. I tried to run past him, but he caught me around the waist and threw me back to the bed. "Where the fuck do you think you're going?"

I cowered up against the headboard. He moved to the bed and grabbed my legs, pulling me down flat on my back. He sat on my stomach and pinned me to the bed. I twisted and turned, trying to get out from underneath him. He reached in his back pocket and pulled out a pair of handcuffs. "Noooooo!" I screamed. He clicked one around my wrist, hooked it through the rails on my headboard and clicked my other wrist into place.

"Why are you doing this?" I cried. "I trusted you!" I pulled against the cuffs, but they just bit into my wrists.

"And I trusted you," he said with a snarl. "And look where that got me. Fucked over, by a fucking lying bitch!"

I looked at him with pleading eyes and shook my head. "You don't have to do this! We can work it out!" I sobbed.

He was still sitting on my stomach, pinning me down. He reached for the top of my tank and ripped it apart down the center. I hadn't put on a bra, so now I was bared to him. He grabbed my breasts and squeezed hard. Then he leaned down and bit my right breast, sinking his teeth into the skin. I yelped out in pain. "These are mine!"

"Help Me!" I screamed. I knew no one would hear me, but I had to try. "Help!" Jake took the pillow and pushed it down over my face.

"Shut the fuck up!" I felt like I was suffocating as I gasped for air under the pillow. Blackness was closing in. I was about to succumb to it when the pillow was lifted from my face. I gasped, trying to suck air back into my lungs. I couldn't breathe through my nose anymore; it was all stuffed up from my crying. I took in quick shallow breaths through my mouth. Then I let out a blood curdling scream.

I watched as his right hand came up and back handed me across my face. I felt my skin slice open as his ring caught it. Then his hand came back, catching the other side of my face with his open palm. "I said to shut the fuck up, bitch!"

I laid there silently crying. I could taste the blood inside my mouth. This was going to happen. There was nothing I could do to stop it.

He moved down my legs, pulling my pants and underwear with him. I tried kicking my legs, but it was no use. "Come on, Kyla. It's not like we've never done it before. I waited a long time to fuck you. I listened to your stupid sob story and waited patiently. You were a little cock tease you know that? Fucking flirting with me, but not giving it up. I put my time in, until you finally gave in. But you gave it to me, I didn't even have to take it. Your pussy is mine now and I'm going to take what's mine." Jake undid his pants and pushed them down his hips.

He grabbed my thighs harshly and pushed them apart. The fight had left me. There was nothing left to do but lay there and take it. Jake tried to push himself inside me, but I was too dry. He spat on his hand and wiped it over my opening. He pushed himself in hard. I let out another yelp and closed my eyes. He thrust into me over and over again, pounding me hard. The tears rolled down my face as I laid there, waiting for it to be over. I felt him tense up and then he collapsed on top of me.

I turned my head and cried into the pillow. Jake pulled out and zipped himself back up. He reached up to the headboard and unlocked the handcuffs. I pulled my arms to my chest and rubbed my wrists.

"This isn't over," he said calmly. "You're still mine." He turned and walked out of my room. I heard the front door open and then close. I pulled the comforter over my naked body and cried myself to sleep.

I woke a couple of hours later. I crawled out of bed and pulled on my pants that were lying on the floor. I found a sweatshirt and put it on too. The apartment was eerily quiet after the destruction that taken place a few hours before.

I walked to the front door and locked it, then moved to the kitchen. My flowers were strewn across the floor. I kneeled down and picked them up. They were wilted and damaged, but I put them in another vase anyway. The necklace had fallen onto a pile of shattered glass. I picked it up and clasped it around my neck. I grabbed some paper towel and a broom and began to clean the mess. I was like a zombie with no emotion. I did what needed to be done. Then I laid down on the kitchen floor and cried some more.

Once I was cried out, I moved to the bathroom. I didn't want to know what I looked like. I shut the door and kept the light off. I stripped my clothes off in the dark and stood naked in front of the full-length mirror on the back of the door. When I was finally ready, I flipped the light switch on.

I barely recognized myself. My right eye was swollen, and I had a gash along my cheek that would probably scar. The area around it was blackening with a bruise. I had a handprint on the left side of my face and a cut on my lip. My right breast had teeth marks where he had sunk them into the skin. Both of my arms were bruised around the biceps where Jake had forcefully grabbed me. I could see the outline of his fingers. My wrists were red and raw from the handcuffs. And I had bruises on both thighs.

I sat on the closed toilet seat and stared at myself. All I could think was that I was glad Tori and Chris wouldn't be home for at least another week. I could hide the bruises on my arms and legs, but my face was another situation. No one could ever know about this. I was so ashamed that I let this happen.

Jake had threatened, *this isn't over*. The hell it wasn't. I was getting a gun. If he came near me again, I would shoot that fucker. I would kill him without regret. I grabbed my hairbrush and threw it at the mirror. The glass cracked, leaving a reflection that was even uglier.

I reached under the sink and pulled out the peroxide and some cotton balls. I started cleaning the gash on my cheek. It stung like a bitch, but it needed to be done. Once I removed the dried blood, the cut wasn't so bad. Just a line about an inch long. Next, I moved to the bite mark and did the same. I cleaned the blood from my lip and turned on the shower. I tried to wash away the filth from my body. I scrubbed between my legs roughly. It hurt, but I didn't care. I reached my fingers inside myself and rinsed away everything that was Jake. Thank God I was on birth control.

I spent the rest of the night, laying on the couch watching *The Christmas Story* over and over again, as the marathon played on. I wasn't really watching. I was formulating my plan. I was going to the gun range the day after Christmas. I was going to get a gun and learn how to use it. I was scared of guns when Jake had taken me, but I wasn't scared anymore. I was pissed.

That fucker would be sorry the next time he tried to rape me. I finally let that word into my mind. That's what he had done to me, and it wouldn't happen again.

I called Tori to wish her a Merry Christmas. I knew if I didn't call her, she would call me. I assured her that I was fine by myself and told her to enjoy her time with her family. I didn't need her worrying and I didn't need her coming home early. She confirmed that they wouldn't be back until after New Year's. That would give me enough time to do some healing and get my gun. I wasn't going to waste time with this. Jake was unpredictable, and I didn't know when he would try to strike again. The sooner I got my gun the better.

The next day was Christmas. I spent most of the day drinking and smoking, trying to bury the shame and the pain. I had just come in from the back patio after another cigarette, when someone knocked on the front door. I momentarily froze, then locked the slider behind me. The knock came again. I hoped to fuck that it wasn't Jake, but who else could it be? I crept to the door and looked out the peephole.

Tyler was standing on my front porch. Shit! He couldn't see me like this. It wasn't even an option. He could never know what happened. I backed away from the door when he knocked again.

"Kyla, I know you're in there. Your car is in the parking lot. Please open the door." His voice wasn't mad or yelling, just pleading. It was silent for a few minutes and then he knocked again. "I'm not going away until we talk. I don't want you alone on Christmas. Open the door please." I slid down against the door and sat on the floor. "That's fine. I'll just sit out here in the cold and wait." I put my hands up over my face and buried my head in them. *Why couldn't he just go away?*

I waited a few minutes and then crept to the window. I could see Ty sitting on the porch, leaning against the door. I wanted nothing more than to open the door and wrap my arms around him. I wanted him to hold me and tell me everything would be all right. I wanted to cry on his shoulder and tell him that I loved him. But I couldn't. Not like this.

My phone rang. I grabbed it off the end table and looked at the screen. It was Tyler. I silenced it quickly and it immediately rang again. I silenced it again and turned it off.

"Kyla, I can hear your phone ringing." He was just talking now, but I could hear him clear as day through the thin door. I sat on the floor on the other side of the door, leaning against it so we were back to back. I held onto the pendant around my neck. "I know you're home. If you won't open the door, please just listen to me. I know I hurt you. I know how wrong I was to treat you like I did. I'm sorry I wasn't there for you when you needed me." The tears started running down my face. "I'm sorry I was an asshole. I'm sorry I walked away from you. You're the best thing that ever happened to me. I'm not the same man without you. I need you. I want back what we had. I miss you so much it hurts. I know we can make this work." I sat there and cried at the words he said. *Why couldn't he have told me all this months ago?*

It was quiet for a long time, and I thought maybe he had left. Then he spoke again. "Ky, I'm missing my heart. I gave it to you a long time ago. I want you to bring it back to me, so it can beat again. I understand why you don't want to talk to me, but I'm not giving up on you. I'm not giving up on us. I love you, Kyla O'Malley." I heard him get up, and then I heard his car start.

I sat leaning against the back of the door crying. "I love you too, Tyler Jackson."

Read the conclusion of Kyla and Tyler's story in
Reviving My Heart.

Song List on Spotify

Torn to Pieces- Pop Evil
Far Away- Nickelback
See You Again- Carrie Underwood
Trying Not to Love You- Nickelback
Ring the Alarm- Beyonce

Acknowledgments

To my husband~ I could have never done this without your love and support. Thank you for putting up with my endless hours of writing, all the take-out dinners, and my never-ending questions about football. I know I made you crazy, but you were a trooper through it all! Thank you for believing in me!

To my daughter~ Thank you for enduring the countless hours I spent writing this book. Your constant questions about what was going to happen next, were inspiring, because even I didn't know. I am giving you permission to read this book when you are 30! Ha Ha!

To Ari, Denise, Kristy, and Amy~ You girls are the best beta readers anyone could ask for! You supported my journey and spent endless hours reading and rereading. Your suggestions, critiques, and encouragement helped me in ways you'll never understand. Thank you for listening to my obsession day after day!

To Jill~ You've been a great friend! When I came to you about my cover designs in frustration, you immediately volunteered to help. Your graphic designs alleviated a ton of stress for me and helped to capture the essence of my books. Thank you for saving the day!

To my readers~ Thank you for supporting me in this journey. Please spread the word if you have enjoyed this book. Without you, writing would still be a dream.

About the Author

Sabrina Wagner lives in Sterling Heights, Michigan. She writes sweet, sassy, sexy romance novels featuring alpha males and the strong women who challenge them.

Sabrina believes that true friends should be treasured, a woman's strength is forged by the fire of affliction, and everyone deserves a happy ending. She enjoys spending time with her family, walking on the beach, cuddling her kittens, and great books. Sabrina is a hopeless romantic and knows all too well that life is full of twists and turns, but the bumpy road is what leads to our true destination.

Want to be the first to learn book news, updates and more? Sign up for my Newsletter.

https://www.subscribepage.com/sabrinawagnernewsletter

Want to know about my new releases and upcoming sales? Stay connected on:

Facebook~Instagram~Twitter~TikTok
Goodreads~BookBub~Amazon

**I'd love to hear from you.
Visit my website to connect with me.**

www.sabrinawagnerauthor.com

Printed in Great Britain
by Amazon